901827

Property of

SMS

Springvalley Middle School

Library Resource Centre

THE
SHADOW
OF FOMOR

THE SHADOW OF FOMOR

TOM McGOWEN

LODESTAR BOOKS

Dutton   New York

Copyright © 1990 by Tom McGowen

Library of Congress Cataloging-in-Publication Data

McGowen, Tom.
  The Shadow of Fomor / Tom McGowen. — 1st ed.
    p.   cm.
  "Lodestar books."
  Summary: Twelve-year-old Rick, visiting his cousin Moira in Ireland, is transported with her into the Middle Kingdom, last haven of the Old Magic, where powerful evil creatures plan to seize total control of both the Kingdom and the real world of Ireland.
  ISBN 0-525-67298-2
  [1. Fantasy. 2. Ireland—Fiction.] I. Title.
PZ7.M47849Sh 1990
[Fic]—dc20   89-37426
                                                                              CIP
                                                                              AC

Published in the United States by Lodestar Books,
an affiliate of Dutton Children's Books,
a division of Penguin Books USA Inc.

Published simultaneously in Canada by Fitzhenry & Whiteside Limited, Toronto

Editor: Rosemary Brosnan   Designer: Richard Granald, LMD
Printed in the U.S.A.   First Edition   10 9 8 7 6 5 4 3 2 1

For all my nieces and nephews—
Don and Bernice, Richard and Jeanne, Sheila and Bob,
Dolores and Frank, John and Chris, Tom and Diane,
Larry and Eve,
Jim and Jan, Chuck and Debbie,
Dennis and Lynn,
Ken and Rosemary,
and Ronnie, Kevin, Laura, and Arlene

Author's Note

A number of words in this story are from the Gaelic language and are presented in standard Gaelic spelling—which makes things difficult for most readers, because a Gaelic word often sounds very different from the way it looks to someone who is used to English spelling. In Gaelic, single letters often have a sound totally different from what they stand for in English, and combinations of letters often stand for sounds that don't even exist in English. As a boy, reading of the adventures of ancient Irish heroes such as Cuchulainn (which is pronounced somewhat like Koo-kull-in, with the second *k* having a soft, scratchy sound far back in the throat), I wrestled with such words as *sidhe* and *cean* not dreaming that they are pronounced as *shee* and *kahn*. To spare my readers from similar struggles, I present here a list of the names and words that appear most frequently in the book, along with phonetic pronunciations as close as possible and the meanings of the words.

Bodach	Boh-thak (with a *th* as in "*th*is")	a goblin
Brollachan	Broh-luh-kan	a monster, a "boneless one"
cailin	kahl-een (colleen)	a young girl
Fomoiri	Foh-moh-ree	a race of monsters
Lair Bhan	Lahr-wan	a name meaning "white mare"
Luchorpan	Loo-ker-pan	one of the "Little Folk"
Neamh Suil	Nahm Shoyl	a name meaning "sky eye"
púca	poo-ka	a malicious spirit that can take the shape of an animal
Roydeg	Roy-theg	a name meaning "bog myrtle" (a plant)
sidhe	shee	a fairy mound

HE STOOD ALONE on the crest of the small hill, awaiting the next onslaught of Queen Maeve's warriors. Three times he had withstood their rush; his shield was dented with the fury of their blows, his spear was reddened with their blood, and the bodies of their slain were piled about his feet. He had bound himself to a tall boulder so that he would not fall, but his arms ached with weariness and he was dizzy from the loss of blood from a score of wounds. He could not hold out much longer. It seemed that the spiteful curse the goddess Mórrígan had put upon him was coming to pass, and he, Cuchulainn of Ulster, mightiest of all Irish warriors, was fighting his last battle . . .

Cuchulainn's face bore a strong resemblance to the face of the tall, slightly skinny twelve-year-old boy who sat on a bumpy stone wall at the bottom of the hill, watching the battle. Actually, the battle was taking place entirely in the boy's imagination, and he had cast himself in the hero's role.

"Rick! Rick McNeese!"

The sound of a distant voice calling his name broke into the boy's fantasy. The warriors vanished from the hilltop. The boy turned his head and saw a blur of color moving up the road toward him. It was his cousin Moira, pedaling up from the farm on a bike. Actually she was his second cousin; her father and his were first cousins. It sure was lucky, he thought, watching her approach, that Dad had an Irish relative who had been urging him for years, in letters, to "come spend a holiday on the old family place." And it was sure great that Dad and Mom had finally accepted the invitation. For an American boy, born and reared in the great, gray city of Chicago and wildly in love with old-world tales of kings, warriors, and magicians, this visit to a green and ancient land was a dream come true.

Moira arrived, sticking out her legs and letting the toes of her shoes scrape the road to brake the bike to a skidding stop. She was a pretty girl, a few months younger than Rick, with shoulder-length, reddish-blond hair and blue-green eyes. Her eyebrows were so pale they were almost invisible, and she had a scattering of freckles beneath both eyes and across the bridge of her nose. It looked as if someone had flung them at her and they had just stuck wherever they landed.

"I just heard a bit o' news," she announced. "Daddy says that someone is movin' into the haunted cottage." Her speech sang with a lilting Irish brogue; she said "whin" for "when," and "loike" for "like," but Rick was growing used to her way of talking, as she was to his.

"A haunted cottage?" He eyed her with interest. "Where?"

She pointed past him. "No more than fifteen or twenty minutes' ride on down the road. It's left over from the time of the great famine, over a hundred years ago. That was when the potato crop went bad and there was starvation everywhere, and millions of people left the country to go to England or America. Cottages were left empty all over the land, and after a time they looked so dark and eerie that most folks felt they must be haunted. Daddy says there were still a lot of them standing when he was a boy, but now there's only this one left in this part of the countryside."

The boy peered eagerly down the road. "Could we go take a look at it?"

She grinned. "I thought you'd want to. That's why I brought Daddy's bike instead of mine. You can pedal and I'll ride on the bar."

She slid from the seat and he took her place, holding the bicycle steady so that she could hop up onto the horizontal crossbar. The bike wavered erratically for a moment as he struggled to get under way, then he picked up speed and they were moving easily down a dirt road. They biked through green and brown fields divided by stone fences like the one on which he had been sitting. The fences were really simple walls of piled up rocks, and Rick had been amused to see that when people wanted to move something from one field to another they just unpiled enough rocks to make a gate, then piled them back up again.

It was easy for him to imagine, as they sped along the empty road, that time had turned back hundreds of years. There wasn't a car, a paved highway, or a high-rise building in sight, and it was so quiet Rick could hear a dog barking far in the distance. He felt a sense of *oldness* practically oozing out of the land, and this charmed him. Imagine all the ancient kings, warriors, and pagan priests who had probably walked, warred, and worshiped right here where he was now!

The ride took a bit longer than the fifteen or twenty minutes that Moira had predicted, but finally the cottage came into view in the distance, set back a short way off the road. It was a low, one-floor structure made of the same kind of stones as the roadside fences, with an old-fashioned thatched roof. Its windows were all tightly shuttered. Beside it, an old, gray, gnarly oak tree lifted twisted limbs to the sky.

When the boy and girl came abreast of the place, Rick brought the bicycle to a stop and Moira hopped down while he straddled the seat, using his legs as a brace to hold the vehicle upright. Like a couple of tourists, the dark-haired boy and coppery-headed girl stood gawking at the little building. It certainly did look rather spooky and forbidding. The roof was pockmarked by several dark, yawning holes, and the chimney was broken, but there were signs of fresh repairs and a ladder was leaning against one wall.

"They're fixing it up already, I guess," Moira murmured in a voice slightly tinged with disappointment. "I suppose they have to, if someone is going to live in it—but it was kind of fun having it sitting here all dark and scary!"

"Yeah, I bet," Rick acknowledged. "Say, I don't suppose we could take a peek inside, could we?"

The girl looked faintly alarmed. "I don't think we should! I mean, it's not really empty anymore, it belongs to somebody now, even if they haven't moved in yet."

"I guess you're right," Rick admitted grudgingly. He was satisfied, though, for he could file the memory of this old, "haunted" cottage alongside those of the ruined abbey, the old castle, and the other interesting things he had seen here so far. "I suppose we ought to be getting back to your folks' farm, anyway. We don't want to be late for supper."

Once again he held the bike while Moira settled herself on the bar. They circled about and began to move back up the road.

4

"Uh-oh, I'm going to have to work now," Rick grunted. "Coming, it was downhill most of the way, but now I'm going to have to pump like heck! Hey—who's that?"

The late afternoon sun was perched low and red in the sky not far off the horizon, and they were heading straight toward it, so their view of what lay ahead of them was fuzzy. But it seemed to them both that someone was standing in the road, directly in their path, about fifty yards ahead—a figure silhouetted in black against the glare of the sun. Rick squinted and Moira cupped a hand over her eyes, and as the distance between them and the figure diminished they saw that the figure appeared to be a person in a long, black robe and pointed hood.

"Who the heck *is* that?" muttered the boy again. He felt oddly uneasy.

"A—a priest?" Moira suggested doubtfully, seeking a rational explanation for the odd sight.

The figure remained absolutely motionless as they neared it, and Rick began to pedal more slowly. He found himself unwilling to pass the strange person. Finally, he coasted to a stop some twenty feet away, holding the bike steady so that Moira wouldn't have to leave her perch. Puzzled and uncertain, the two young people stared at the apparition.

They couldn't tell whether it was a man or a woman. The black robe hung to its feet and the hood covered the upper part of its face, leaving the lower portion in shadow. It was as still as a statue, and Moira suddenly realized, with a little thrill of terror, that not even the folds of its robe were moving, although a strong breeze was stirring the grass in the nearby field!

Slowly, the figure's right arm began to move. It lifted and the long, loose sleeve of the robe gradually slid back to reveal

5

a thin, ivory-white hand and wrist. The hand was extended toward the boy and girl, a bony finger pointing at them, and they felt a sudden chill, as one does when the sun abruptly goes behind a cloud and a rain-laden breeze springs up. Rick tried to walk the bicycle backward but found to his horror that he seemed rooted to the ground, unable to move.

The figure began to come down the road toward them. It seemed to glide, as if its feet were not touching the ground. Then, somewhere in the field behind the stone fence that edged one side of the road, a dog barked loudly and a man's voice called out something. The robed figure flickered and vanished.

Rick heard himself say "uh!" in a shocked grunt, and Moira gasped. Moments later, a short, stocky Irish farmer with a large dog ambling at his heels strode out from an opening in the fence and crossed the road to the opposite field. He glanced toward the two youngsters and flipped his hand in a casual wave to them. They realized that it must have been the sound of his voice and the barking of his dog that had caused the strange, menacing figure to disappear.

"What was it?" Moira asked shakily. "A ghost?"

The boy had to wet his lips to answer. "I don't know. But let's get out of here!"

Desperately, he pumped hard on the pedals to urge the bike into motion. Legs churning, he drove it up the road as fast as he could make it move.

≈2≈

"MOIRA, GIRL, YOU'RE HARDLY TOUCHING YOUR SUPPER. That's not like you. Is anything the matter?"

Mrs. O'Keefe looked at her daughter with mild concern. Moira had done little more than toy absent-mindedly with her food since the O'Keefes and McNeeses had begun the evening meal.

"Rick doesn't seem to be his usual starving self, either," remarked the boy's mother. "I hope you kids didn't ride into town and fill yourselves up with candy or snacks this afternoon!"

Rick and Moira exchanged glances, and a silent agreement passed between them.

"Something happened this afternoon, Mum," said Moira, putting down her fork with a decisive thump. "Rick and I were coming back from looking at the haunted cottage and we saw—we saw something terribly strange and scary!"

Everyone at the table stared at her for a few moments, then all eyes seemed to swing automatically to Rick.

"We both saw it," he acknowledged. "It looked like a man in a black robe and hood standing in the middle of the road. And while we were looking at him, he—well, he *disappeared*."

Moira's brother, Tim, who was twenty and helped his father on the farm, said slowly, "Now, do you mean that he just ran away quick, or that he truly disappeared?"

"He disappeared!" Rick and Moira answered together.

There was total silence. Rick's parents stared at their son, Mrs. O'Keefe studied the ceiling with a worried expression, and Mr. O'Keefe and Tim continued to eat, but their expressions were thoughtful.

"That's a pretty tall order, Rick," Mr. McNeese said at last. "You two sure you're not just having fun with us?"

"No, Dad," Rick said firmly, and Moira shook her head so vigorously that her hair swung across her face.

Mr. O'Keefe put down his fork and cleared his throat. "I don't think they're trying to kid us, Jack. I know that most Americans don't much believe in such things, but it's a fact that queer things do sometimes happen in this country. And it's a fact that some mighty queer things have been happening right around here of late."

Tim nodded. "They have, that!"

"What sorts of things?" Rick's father asked.

Mr. O'Keefe shifted uneasily in his chair and quickly glanced from Moira to Rick. "I've no wish to be frightening the young ones, but perhaps it's just as well if they know that they're not the only ones to be seeing strange things. Well, then"—he rested his elbows on the table and pressed his fingertips together—"the first thing happened the day after you began your holiday here. It was early in the morning, and Jimmy Finucane and Sean Nolan were in Jimmy's horse-drawn jaunting cart that he uses for taking tourists around. They were driving to market in the town of Cairwick. Now the road to Cairwick passes by an old, tall tree, standing right at the edge of the road, that's called the

8

Fairy Thorn, because, according to old tales, it was once sacred to the fairy folk. Jimmy, who told me about this himself, says they were about a dozen meters from the tree when all at once the horse gave a snort and tried to back up right into the cart. Jimmy says that he cried out to the horse, 'What the devil is wrong with you?', but then he saw there was a person standing in the road by the tree, although he swears no one had been there until that very second. The person looked like a man in a long, black robe with a hood over his head."

"Just like what we saw!" Moira exclaimed.

Her father nodded, then continued in his soft Irish brogue. "Jimmy says that the person or whatever it was never moved a muscle, but the Fairy Thorn tree was twisting and swaying as if it were caught in a great wind—even though there wasn't enough of a breeze in the air to ruffle a man's hair, Jimmy swears! He and Sean sat in the cart with their mouths hanging open, and then, just like a candle going out, the figure in the robe vanished, the tree stopped moving, and the horse became as calm as if nothing at all had happened. But Jimmy and Sean decided they weren't going to pass that tree just then for all the bargains in Cairwick, so they turned the cart around and went home."

Mr. and Mrs. McNeese sat in shocked silence, trying to digest this strange tale. After a few moments, Tim broke into the stillness with a self-conscious clearing of his throat.

"Then there was the thing that happened to Paddy Grogan last Friday," he said. "That was when you were sight-seeing off in Dublin. It was late afternoon, and Paddy was coming home from a visit to old Mrs. Willis, who's been sick. He spied three people standing in a field ahead of him.

9

Paddy's eyes are none too good, and he says he thought at first they were women in black dresses, with shawls over their heads. He wondered what they were doing, for he says they were standing in a sort of triangle, facing one another and not moving or talking that he could see. He went toward them to find out what it was all about, and when he got close enough he saw they weren't women in dresses at all, they appeared to be men in long, black, hooded robes." Tim nodded at Rick and Moira. "Yes, just like what you and Sean and Jimmy all saw. Only, Paddy got a look at their faces, and he says that he'll never forget them as long as he lives! White as chalk they were, he says, and with eyes like colorless chips of ice. He let out a yell and skedaddled away from there as fast as ever he could!"

Finishing his story, Tim reached for his water glass. Mr. O'Keefe spoke again.

"So there are two strange things that have happened within just a week's time to people I know well, and now a third thing that's happened to my own flesh and blood. It means something, Jack and Betty, believe me it does. Here in Ireland we've come to know that sometimes there's a kind of breaking loose of things that maybe shouldn't be around today—*old* things, that were driven into the woods and hills long ago. We call them by a lot of different names. The Little People, the Earth Folk, Fairies . . ." His voice trailed off into silence.

Mr. McNeese rubbed his chin. "Well, why do you think they're—uh—'breaking loose' now?"

"Paddy Grogan thinks," Tim volunteered, "that they're looking for something."

Rick's father leaned back in his chair, his eyes serious. "I hardly know what to say, Gerry. I've never been one to

10

believe in ghosts and such things, and I suppose I'd be inclined to smile at these stories you and Tim have told us, if it weren't for the fact that our own two kids apparently saw something pretty weird. I just don't know."

Mr. O'Keefe nodded to show that he understood. "As I said, I know it isn't easy for a Yank to believe in such things, Jack, even if he's a full-blooded Irishman like you. But if you'd been born and reared here, instead of in America, you'd believe too, just as most of us do. This is an old, old land, Jack, and maybe there's still a bit of magic lying about in it."

Mrs. O'Keefe stood up. "I'll be bringing in the pudding now," she said, referring to the dessert. Rick leaned back in his chair, his thoughts whirling. He had, there seemed little doubt, encountered a genuine supernatural creature right out of the oldest legends of Ireland. Surely, nothing more could happen on this wonderful vacation to top that!

❧3❧

THE NEXT MORNING DAWNED so bright, blue-skied, and full of promise that to both Rick and Moira the strange encounter with the robed figure seemed remote and almost dreamlike. All that Rick could think about was that there were still six days left of his vacation in Ireland, and lots of things left to see. At breakfast, when Mrs. O'Keefe reminded Moira that she wanted her to go to the nearby town of Ballymor on an errand, the boy quickly volunteered to go along. He hadn't yet seen the little village close up and wanted to explore it.

With Rick on Mr. O'Keefe's bicycle and Moira on her own, they started out. But they hadn't gone a quarter of a mile when they became aware of a chugging, wheezing noise growing louder behind them; peering over their shoulders, they saw an ancient truck advancing up the road. They stopped and squeezed to one side to let it pass, but it coughed to a standstill beside them. A tiny man with a red, wrinkled face stuck his head out of the driver's window.

"Are ye for Ballymor, Moira girl?" he shouted. She nodded yes, and he continued, "Then I'll save yer legs and be glad for yer company. Throw yer bikes in the back and hop in."

Moira hesitated, glancing at Rick. He shrugged, dis-

12

mounted, and slid first his bike and then hers into the back of the truck. The girl clambered up into the cab and he followed her. The little man regarded him with interest. "Now, you must be Gerry O'Keefe's cousin's boy from America, eh? Me name's Parnell, Michael Parnell." He let out the clutch, and with a shiver and cough, the truck lurched on its way.

It quickly became obvious that Mr. Michael Parnell had sought company because he liked to talk. He fired questions at Rick, launched into a monologue about his desire to visit America someday, then began questioning Moira about a local matter in which her father was involved. Rick let his attention wander to the countryside that was rolling past. All around were green checkerboards of fields, spread out in a broad panorama. The truck passed a herd of grazing sheep, then a cluster of cows. In the far distance Rick could see a grayish huddle of stone that looked as if it might be another old, ruined castle or abbey. Have to ask Moira about that, he thought. Then the truck passed a high, swollen, green mound that looked much too evenly contoured to be an ordinary hill. Have to ask about that, too, he told himself.

"Well, here's Ballymor," announced Michael Parnell, jerking Rick's attention back, and he saw that the truck was approaching a huddle of houses. "I'll drop ye off here, for I'm goin' on to Innisfree," Parnell said.

At the edge of the town they hopped down from the cab, retrieved their bikes from the back of the truck, and watched the archaic vehicle splutter off. Then, walking their bikes along, they made their way to a little store where Moira bought the spool of thread that was the object of her errand.

Rick was charmed by the village. It consisted of a few houses, a tavern (called a pub), a drugstore (called a pharmacy) in which nothing *but* medicines and chemicals were sold, and the general store in which one seemed able to buy anything from canned goods to small articles of clothing. A short distance outside the village rose the steeple of an old church, at the back of which was a graveyard where the people of Ballymor and vicinity had buried their dead for generations.

After making her purchase, Moira indulged her cousin's desire to explore. She led him through all the streets of the village, pointing out the homes of family friends, then to the graveyard, where she showed him the resting places of her grandmother, grandfather, a great-grandfather, and a great-great grandmother. Rick, who didn't even know where any of his great-great grandparents had lived, was impressed.

"That's a neat little town," he commented when they were again on the road pedaling their bikes toward home. "I wouldn't mind living in a quiet old place like that."

"*I'd* like to live in Chicago, or another big, busy American city like you do!" Moira declared.

At that moment Rick caught sight, in the distance, of the green mound he had noticed as they were in the truck heading for Ballymor. "Say, what is that thing up ahead, Moira? It doesn't look like an ordinary hill."

"Oh, no, that's a *sidhe*," Moira replied. "It's supposed to be a fairy hill—an entrance to Fairyland. Mr. Savage, the schoolteacher, says it's really a tomb that prehistoric people built thousands of years ago to bury a great chief in."

"Wow!" Rick exclaimed. "Let's go look at it up close."

Moira gnawed nervously at her lip. The stories her father

and brother had told at the supper table came flooding back into her mind, and she wasn't sure she wanted to get too close to anything that was so definitely linked to the Earth Folk. But as they came abreast of the mound, Rick steered his bicycle to a stop and leaned it up against the ever-present stone fence, so she reluctantly followed suit.

The boy hopped to a sitting position on the fence, swung his legs around, and dropped onto the meadow on the other side. Fifty yards away in the center of the meadow, the great green mound awaited him. He jogged toward it.

Halting at the foot of the *sidhe,* he stood with hands on hips and stared up at it. It looked like nothing more than a smooth, grass-covered hill, but now that he knew what it really was, the awe and mystery of it reached out to him.

"Come on!" With long strides he hurried up the slope, intent upon seeing the other side and examining every inch of the ancient construction. As he reached the crest he stood outlined against the brilliant blue sky for a moment, then he dropped from Moira's sight as he headed down the reverse slope. She hurried to join him.

Halfway down the other side he paused, waiting for her to catch up. He was grinning with pleasure, but Moira felt uneasy. A tiny dent of a frown creased her forehead. She had been on the *sidhe* many times before, but now she felt oddly fearful. Turning to glance back up at the crest, she realized that she and Rick could not be seen from the road. She peered sharply about at the fields that bordered the meadow; they were empty, without a person in sight. Moira suddenly felt terribly alone and vulnerable.

"Rick," she said, nervously, and then her voice rose in a terrified shriek. "Rick!"

For, three black-robed figures had materialized silently

around them. Their hoods were pushed back so that their faces were visible—faces that were chalk-white even to the lips, and with eyes that shone like mirrors reflecting sunlight.

Instinctively, the boy and girl clutched at each other. Like the first time they had encountered one of these creatures, they felt strangely rooted to the ground, unable to move. The air around them became chilled. The black-robed beings flowed silently toward them from three sides.

And then—suddenly—the boy and girl winked right out of existence, vanishing completely. Where they had stood clutching each other was now empty ground. The white-faced creatures recoiled in surprise, hissing like angry snakes!

❧ 4 ❧

TO RICK IT FELT AS IF THE EARTH had suddenly opened up beneath his feet. He had a momentary sensation of falling, then he found himself sprawling among a mass of dead leaves and soft, springy moss.

Confused, he scrambled wildly to his feet, expecting to be seized at any moment by the shining-eyed creatures, and ready to punch, kick, and claw to fight his way free of them. But as his eyes focused on his surroundings he gave an involuntary shout of astonishment and stood staring about, wide-eyed and open-mouthed.

The black-robed figures were gone. The *sidhe* and the countryside around it were gone. The open sky above was gone. He was in a clearing in the midst of what seemed to be an immense forest.

But it was like no forest he had ever seen except possibly in his dreams. It *glowed*. The tree trunks that rose like pillars all around him had the sheen of silver, and the roof of leaves overhead glistened like a mass of deep-green emeralds. From above, a pale green light filled with dancing golden sparks slanted down among the tree trunks, and the fallen leaves that lay on the forest floor glinted like burnished copper.

Rick became aware of Moira beside him, on her hands

17

and knees, staring at these strange surroundings in shock. "Where are we?" she said with a gasp. "Where are *they*? What's happened?"

"Don't be frightened, young ones," said a pleasant, soothing voice. "There's naught to fear, now."

Their heads turned toward the sound. They beheld a figure out of a fairy tale!

A man stood between two trees at the edge of the clearing. He was no more than two feet tall, and he had a lumpy, potatolike nose, large ears that came to distinct points, and a face as wrinkled as a raisin, with a white fringe of beard. His clothes were as fantastic as the forest. A blouselike jacket the color of russet autumn leaves hung to his knees, his legs were clad in skintight breeches of dark green, and his feet were shod in ankle-high boots of soft yellow leather with curled-up, pointed toes. A pale green hood covered his head. He was bent forward slightly from the weight of a bulky leather sack that he carried slung over one shoulder.

Moira instantly concluded, "This is Faeryland! And ye're an elf!"

The little man's eyes became nearly invisible in a mass of wrinkles as he smiled at her. "Not exactly, *cailin*. To be precise, I'm a Luchorpan, though I think that word has gotten a bit twisted in your world, and they call it 'leprechaun.' "

"You're a leprechaun?" Rick asked, still half-dazed.

The little man clucked his tongue. "Now, now, and didn't I just tell ye the correct word is *Luchorpan*?" he said with mock severity. Then his face grew serious and sympathetic. "Ah, ye poor young things, ye're addled and frightened still. Ye've been hounded by the enemy and snatched out o' yer

18

own world and ye've no idea at all what 'tis all about. Sit down and let me explain."

Gratefully, Rick and Moira sank cross-legged to the soft ground. They were unaware of it, but by his voice and manner the little man had calmed them, dispelling the hysterical terror that they felt at the strange suddenness of events. He strode into the clearing, heaved the bag from his shoulder with a grunt, and using it as a backrest, sat down with his legs stretched out in front of him and his hands in his lap.

"First," he said, "what may I call ye?"

"Moira O'Keefe."

"Rick McNeese."

He nodded. "Moira is a beautiful old name that I know well. 'Rick' is new to me, though. But I like it. It has the sound of a sword being drawn from its scabbard. And you two may call me Nion.

"Now." He settled back more comfortably, throwing one leg casually over the other. "Ye want to know where ye are and how ye got here, and why the Fomoiri were after ye. Well, as to where ye are, you're in the Coil Mor, the Great Forest of the Middle Kingdom, which your people often do call the Land of Faery."

Rick leaned forward. "But where *is* it? Are we inside the *sidhe*, somehow?"

Nion pursed his lips. "The *sidhe* is an opening between your world and this one," he answered. "The Middle Kingdom is part of your world, in a way, yet it is outside your world. It is the home of your world's legends and the last haven of the Old Magic. It is the place where time never moves." He smiled apologetically. "More than that I'm afraid I cannot tell ye. It is a hard thing to explain, and I'm not sure I quite understand it myself!

"Now, as to why you are here," he continued, "ye were brought here by Druid magic, to keep you from falling into the hands of the Fomoiri." His lips twisted in a grimace, as if the last word he spoke had put a foul taste in his mouth.

"The Fomoiri?" Moira stared at him. "Are those the ones who were trying to grab us on the *sidhe*?"

The Luchorpan nodded. "Let me tell ye a story, young ones. Long ago—and I mean *long* ago, when your ancestors dressed in animal skins and made their tools out of stone and wood—this place, as well as your land of Ireland, were ruled by the Fomoiri. Now, the Fomoiri have assumed the shapes of humans, but they are not human. They came from somewhere out of the eternal darkness, and darkness is what they worship. They have the power to cause fogs, twilight, and bone-chilling cold, and they hate warmth, light, and happiness! Their rule was one of darkness and pain and fear and blood! From the people of Ireland they took a yearly tax—two-thirds of all the food that was produced and one-third of all the babes that were born." He grimaced again. "That was a time of misery and terror for your people, and not much of a better one for mine, for the Fomoiri had us marked for total extermination, and we had to stay in almost constant hiding.

"Then, one day, out of the sea in shining ships came the ones known as the Tuatha De Danaan, the Children of Danu. They were creatures of light and life and song and joy—all the things that the Fomoiri hated!"

Moira had risen to her knees, her face alive with excitement. "Why, I know this story! It's an old Irish legend. Mr.

20

Moynahan read it to us at school. The Danaan drove the Fomoiri out of Ireland after a great battle!"

Nion nodded. "Aye, a great and terrible battle." He closed his eyes and began to chant what sounded like a fragment of some ancient epic poem:

"Fearful indeed was the thunder
which rolled over the battlefield—
the shouts of the warriors,
the breaking of the shields,
the clashing of the swords,
and the sighing flight of the spears!"

He opened his eyes, regarding the boy and girl, who were listening intently. "Scores of Danaan warriors were slain. Even their king himself, Nuada of the Silver Hand, was slain, along with Macha, the warrior-woman who was his queen. The outcome of the battle was in doubt.

"But then, Lugh the Fiery One hurled himself into the Fomoiri, dodging their swords and spears, making his way straight toward their king, Balor of the Killing Eye. Balor turned his deadly, pale eye upon Lugh, but could not face him, for Lugh's own eyes were glowing with the light of the sun, his body was glowing like molten gold, and sparks of flame were shooting from his red hair! From his belt, Lugh took forth the Tahthlum, the Stone of Light, and with all his power, flung it at Balor. It struck the Fomor and burst with a dazzling glare of light that spread over the whole field of battle, blinding the Fomoiri and bewildering them. Then the Fomoiri host broke in fear, and fled out of your world into this one, and withdrew into their last refuge, an island shrouded in darkness, lying in the cold sea far to the north.

21

And all the evil creatures that had been allied to the Fomoiri were hunted and harried out of your world as well, by the Danaan, and driven into bogs and wild moors and sunless caverns here in the Middle Kingdom. The Danaan, too, left your world to be ruled by its own kind of people, and came here and built their shining cities. So, light came to this place as well as to yours, and light has ruled here since that time. For thousands upon thousands of years the Fomoiri huddled on their bleak island in fear and silence, and their scattered evil creatures lurked fearfully in their remote hiding places, and all was well."

He sighed. "But now, of late, the Danaan mages have become aware of a stealthy stirring of their ancient enemies. The Fomoiri seem to have built up their strength and power once more and are beginning to do things. They have cast a dark shadow over the entire northland of the Middle Kingdom, a shadow into which the Danaan mages cannot see. The ancient evil allies of Fomor have been creeping out of their hiding places and making their way into the shadow. Something is going on there, and the Danaan fear that the Fomoiri may be making ready to come forth and seek to regain their rule. They have become so strong and sure of themselves that some of them have even entered *your* world again."

Moira looked at Rick. "They must be the ones that we and Paddy Grogan and the others saw! But why would such powerful magical creatures go to a little place like Ballymor? It's nothing special. What could they be wanting there?"

She had asked the question out of idle curiosity, not really expecting an answer. But, after hesitating for a moment, Nion gave her one that astonished both her and Rick.

"They want you, young ones," he said.

Rick's jaw dropped. "Us?"

"We do not know whether it is both of you they want or just one," said Nion. "But for some eight days now, we have known they were seeking something in the area of that little village you call Ballymor, and two days ago we learned it was you they sought."

"But why?" Moira asked. "Why would ancient magical folk be after a couple of kids?"

Rick looked imploringly at the Luchorpan. "It doesn't make any sense! I never even heard of these Fomoiri until now. And I'm not even *from* Ballymor, or anyplace in Ireland. I'm an American, from across the ocean. How could they know anything about me?"

Nion tugged off his hood and rubbed the thatch of grayish hair that was revealed. "I cannot answer your questions. It is our hope that when some of the Danaan Druids can talk with you they may be able to discover what it is that the Fomoiri want of you." He leaned forward and put a gentle hand on Moira's shoulder. "But don't be afraid. We'll keep you safe from them here."

Rick and Moira quickly glanced at each other. They had both thought that they would soon be able to go back to their own world, to Moira's father's farm. But it seemed from what Nion had just said that they might be kept in this Middle Kingdom for some time yet.

"Aren't we—won't we be going home soon, then?" Moira asked, somewhat tremulously.

The Luchorpan shook his head. "Don't you see, mocushla, that there's no safety for you there? The Fomoiri nearly had ye today, and if you went back they'd have ye for sure, quick as a wink! You wouldn't even be safe in your own

23

house. I'm sorry, I truly am, but ye cannot go back to your world just yet."

"Our folks will be worried!" Rick protested.

The Luchorpan eyed him thoughtfully. "Perhaps I can get a message to them, assuring them you're safe," he suggested. "There are ways I might do that."

He glanced about. The light that streamed in among the trees had taken on a reddish cast, and the silvery tree trunks were touched with purple. Shadows were inching out from beneath the trees, stretching, touching, and flowing together to form dark patches on the forest floor.

"The sun is going down," Nion observed. "Sometime after moonrise a friend will join us. His name is Faol. In the morning, he and I will take you to a place where ye'll be as safe and snug as a cricket on a hearth. Now"—reaching around, he pulled the leather bag from behind him and placed it on his knees—"let us have a bit of supper."

He began to lift delicacies out of the bag and hand them around. Rick and Moira found themselves each with a small roasted fowl of some sort, little loaves of delicious, crusty bread, chunks of tangy white cheese, and little silver goblets into which Nion poured sparkling pale green liquid from a silver flask. Having eaten nothing since morning, the boy and girl gobbled up these delights with gratitude.

As they ate, the twilight thickened and the forest darkened until Moira and Rick could see each other and the Luchorpan only as dim, indistinct forms. Then the moon rose high enough so that pale silver light bathed the tops of the trees and dripped down wherever it found an opening, to push aside shadows and spill into silvery-gray pools on the ground. The clearing in which Nion, Moira, and Rick sat was a circle of silver.

Abruptly, a figure stepped out of the darkness and into the ring of light. It was a tall man with pale hair that fell to his shoulders and glowed like a halo in the moonlight. A glinting tunic of metal-scaled armor hung to his knees and a long cloak flowed from his shoulders. On his left arm was a round shield covered with an intricate pattern, and in his right hand he held a long spear. The hilt of a sword, in a scabbard fastened to his back, projected up over his right shoulder.

"Ah, Faol," said Nion, leaning back with his hands on his thighs. "Ye're welcome. Sit down and—"

"No time," the man interrupted sharply. "Bands of Bo-dachs have been moving into the forest since sundown. They're hunting us. We must flee quickly!"

❧5❧

NION LEAPED TO HIS FEET in obvious alarm, and the boy and girl did the same.

"What are Bodachs?" Rick wondered aloud.

"Servants of the Fomoiri," the tall Faol answered him. "Be glad 'twas I found you first and not they. Give me your hand."

Rick extended his hand, which Faol took and held in a firm grip. Without any warning, the boy found himself trotting at Faol's side, trying to keep up with the warrior's long, loose stride. Moira and Nion, also hand in hand, were close behind. The four quickly moved out of the moonlit clearing and plunged into the full blackness of the forest.

Rick felt almost as if he had gone blind. The darkness was like a thick swath of black velvet covering his eyes, and he knew that without Faol's guidance he would be blundering into trees and tripping over roots and bushes. Apparently Faol could see far better than he in this blackness. Nion could too, it seemed, for he was leading Moira along with confidence.

Moira leaned to one side until she judged that her mouth was approximately at the Luchorpan's ear. "Nion," she whispered, "is Faol a Danaan?"

"Aye," the little man answered, and said nothing more.

Moira straightened up, dazzled by a feeling of wonder. The ancient legends of her land had come to life and she was walking among them!

"Where are we going?" Rick asked.

"To a place of safety for you," the Danaan replied. "The city of Murias, the greatest and oldest of our strongholds."

"Well, look," said Rick, pursuing the thought that had been worrying him for some time, "even when we get there, this trouble with these Fomoiri guys won't just stop, will it? It sounds to me like there might even be a war with them!"

"I fear you are right," Faol answered, his voice grim.

"Well, would Moira and I have to stay in this Murias until the war's over?" Rick persisted.

There was a short silence, as if Faol were pondering his answer. "Probably," he acknowledged. "For your sakes as much as for ours. If we put you back into your world the Fomoiri could seize you, and you may be a weapon for them to use against us. We do not know just why it is they want you so badly."

Rick considered the situation. A war could last a long time—years might pass before the Danaan won and Moira and he could be safely sent back into their world. He could imagine that he and Moira might well be given up for dead by their parents after so long a time. His mother and father undoubtedly would have gone back home to America by then. And what if they moved to some other part of the country while he was stuck here in the Middle Kingdom? Would he be able to find them?

"Say, Faol," he began, "what would happen if—"

"*Anogt!*" The warrior's low, sharp exclamation cut off Rick's question. Even though the boy didn't understand the word, the urgency of Faol's tone made him stop talking and come to an instant halt. Moira and Nion also stopped at once.

"Off to the left, behind us," said Faol in the thinnest of whispers. "Do you see?"

Rick and Moira peered into the darkness. After a few moments they became aware of tiny points of reddish light, like bright stars, moving erratically, vanishing and reappearing. "What are they?" asked Moira.

"Bodachs," murmured Nion, "moving among the trees with torches."

"Aye, they must have come into the forest from the west as well as the north," Faol commented, still whispering. "Come, we must move quickly. And let us now keep silent!"

Rick found himself trying to walk rapidly on tiptoe, putting his feet down as gently as he could. Even so, the *shush-shush-shush* of their movement through the carpet of leaves underfoot seemed agonizingly loud. He prayed that the sound wouldn't carry far enough for the torchbearers to hear.

Moving through the blackness, knowing that some terrible, unknown enemy was pursuing him, the boy began to feel as if he were trapped in a nightmare. In one of his books at home, one that had long been his favorite, several chapters described a long journey through a spooky, danger-filled forest. He had always liked those chapters best; each time he read them he had thought of what fun such an adventure would be. Well, here he was, having a genuine adventure, tiptoeing through a black and silver faery forest in a strange world with a bunch of fearsome creatures on his trail. But it was most definitely not fun—he was thoroughly scared! He realized now that reading about danger while safe at home was far more "thrilling" than really *being* in danger.

The forest no longer seemed as totally dark as it had been. Rick thought he could detect the vague shapes of tree trunks as black columns against an even blacker background. Overhead there were faint gray glimmers, as openings among tree branches let an occasional trickle of moonlight through. He turned his head to test this new-found night vision and saw, off to the right, probably no more than some two hundred yards away, more flickering reddish lights.

"Faol!" he whispered as softly but forcefully as he could, to call the man's attention to the danger.

"I see them," Faol whispered back.

From behind came a tiny whisper from Moira. "They're all around us!"

Rick peered back over his shoulder. There were, indeed, lights stretched out behind them now, as well as on both sides. His heart began to pound.

It seemed to be getting lighter. Was that possible? The tree trunks all around were no longer black columns but distinct shafts of gray. Rick found that he could even make out branches and clumps of leaves. Faol was a shadowy shape beside him, and Moira and Nion were dim figures behind. He realized that the trees were farther apart and that the moonlight was becoming increasingly brighter. Were they coming to the edge of the forest?

But it was not the forest's edge, it was merely a broad clearing; beyond it in the distance was a wall of blackness that marked the beginning of the forest again. The moon shone full on the clearing, a wide meadow of knee-high grass and herbs, like a little island of silver in a great black ocean.

They stopped at the edge of the clearing. Faol released

29

Rick's hand and turned to scan the lights that flickered among the trees in a wide semicircle behind them.

"If we can cross this clearing before they reach its edge, we may be safe," he whispered. "Now let us run, and may our feet have wings!"

He launched himself forward. Moira and Rick were a split second behind him, running with the swiftness of youth, but white-bearded Nion was even with them, moving with surprising speed.

Then, suddenly, they became aware of flickers of light sparkling all along the length of blackness toward which they were running. Torches were moving toward them out of the far edge of the forest.

Faol, a few paces ahead of his three companions, abruptly stopped and stood, feet planted far apart, staring toward the moving lights.

"It is no use," he said in a normal tone of voice. "They have us surrounded. They have driven us to this place as if we were hares! They must have entered the forest on all sides."

"What will they do to us?" Moira sounded as frightened as Rick felt.

"Before they can do anything, they must take us," remarked Nion. Looking at him, Rick and Moira saw that a short, broad-bladed sword was glittering in his hand.

"Aye," growled the Danaan. "There are surely scores of them, but if Mórrígan, goddess of battle, favors us, we may be able to drive them off. They are cowardly creatures, at best." Reaching up to his shoulder he grasped the hilt of his sword and slid the blade free of the scabbard that was strapped to his back. It came out with a soft rasping sound,

30

and he held it hilt-first toward Rick. "Now you must do a warrior's work, lad."

With a feeling of complete unreality, Rick took the sword. Surely, this wasn't actually happening! Surely he wasn't going to have to hack and stab at someone! The blade glinted in the moonlight as he hefted it uncertainly. It was far too heavy for him to wield with one hand, so he closed both fists around the hilt, holding it like a baseball bat.

Faol had now stooped over and was fumbling at the top of one of his boots. He drew forth a wicked-looking dirk that had been sheathed between his boot and leg and handed it to Moira. "This is the best I can do for you, *cailin,* but it is a sharp fang and if you strike hard enough, one bite will do."

Rick was astounded at the way the Danaan seemed to automatically assume that a couple of twelve-year-old kids would be willing and able to fight and kill somebody! Obviously, the people of this strange world thought about things a little differently from the kind of people he knew. Maybe in this world kids were expected to be able to fight, using deadly weapons, if the need arose. And he had to admit that there seemed to be such a need, right now. From what he had heard of the Bodachs and from what he'd seen of the icy-eyed Fomoiri, he certainly didn't want to fall into their hands. Still . . . he stared doubtfully at the sword he was holding.

Moira took the dirk Faol was offering her and looked at it for a moment. Then she gave a kind of toss of her head, pushed her hair back, and set her jaw. Rick would have bet that she was as scared as he was, but it was obvious that she intended to fight like fury. Okay, he decided he would do the same—only he hoped that his legs, which were shaking

31

badly, wouldn't give way at the last minute! Gritting his teeth, he swung the sword in an arc, as if he were swinging at a fast pitch in a baseball game. The blade sliced through the air with a *swoosh*.

"Ah!" Faol, who had been watching the two of them, sounded pleased. "We have two hearty battle comrades, Nion!" He tossed his spear lightly into the air and caught it, one-handed, in thrusting position. "I would let one of you young ones use my shield, but it was fashioned for a strong man's arm, and I do not think you could hold it. I will cover us all with it as best I can."

The flickering torches were all around them now, in a ring of glowing orange that was rapidly closing in on them. "Let us form a circle, that we may cover one another's backs," said Faol.

Rick felt his heart beating so fast and hard that he was sure the others must hear it, too. A thought struck him, and he pulled his good luck charm from his pocket, kissed it for luck, and put it back. It was just a round chunk of reddish metal that he'd found down in his basement a couple of years ago, and he didn't really much believe in it, but he figured he needed all the help he could get! He noticed that Moira's lips were moving, apparently in prayer, and silently he joined her.

The torches moved steadily nearer, and the four could hear the muffled shuffling of many feet treading through the meadow grass. They could also begin to make out arms, shoulders, and gleaming heads, illumined by the flaring torchlight.

"Ugh!" Moira exclaimed with loathing as she clearly saw the Bodachs. They looked like shrunken mummies, with the wrappings removed. They were about three feet tall, with incredibly scrawny limbs and dull gray skin that looked as if it had shriveled up and become tightly stretched over their skeletons. They were as hairless as snakes, and wore only skirtlike garments of animal skin. Each of them carried a crudely made leather shield and slim spear tipped with a point of whitish stone. In the background, looming over the dwarfish bodies, were several enormously tall, yellow-skinned creatures, indistinct in the shadows.

"There are Brollachans with them," muttered Nion.

"Aye," said Faol, and spat. "The Fomoiri have swept up every unclean creature they could find to use against us, it seems."

At a distance of about twenty yards, the horde of creatures halted, surrounding the four with a tight-packed ring of gray, scrawny bodies. There was not a sound from them once they stopped moving, and the meadow was so quiet that the far-off hooting of an owl could be clearly heard, and Rick and Moira became aware of the buzz and whir of countless crickets.

Then, a voice like a rusty hinge wheezed, "Danaan?"

"*Apair,*" growled Faol.

The rusty hinge creaked out a string of words that were meaningless to Rick, but he saw Moira suddenly stiffen and glance with frightened eyes at Faol. He realized the Bodach must be speaking Gaelic, the ancient language of Ireland, which he knew Moira understood somewhat.

"He has said that it is not Nion nor I that they want," Faol translated. "They offer to let us go free if we give them you, to be taken to the Fomoiri. They would rather not fight if they can avoid it, you see. As I told you, they are cowardly things."

Raising his voice he shouted an answer that made Moira

grin and raise her hand to her lips as if she were faintly shocked. Whatever the Danaan had said, it seemed to enrage the Bodachs. A ripple of motion swept through the ring of bodies.

"Danaan!" screeched the rusty hinge with distinct anger. "*Amairg dhuit! Apail! Apail!*"

"*Apail! Apail!*" echoed the others, with voices like the croakings of monstrous, slimy toads.

"They are working themselves up to a fighting rage," Faol said softly. "Only the boldest will come at us first. If we can beat them back, we have a good chance."

The little monsters were all shrieking now, and some of them were doing a weird, shuffling sort of dance. Rick suddenly realized that when the Bodachs charged he might die, for even though they wanted to take him and Moira captive, anything might happen once spears were being thrusted. He remembered reading of how legendary warriors such as Cuchulainn had often faced death in battle gaily, but he realized now that most real people didn't face sudden death at all gaily. Faol and Nion certainly didn't appear gay—their lips were tight and their eyes hard. Moira's face was pale and wide-eyed. As for Rick, he was scared—so scared his stomach hurt and his mouth felt as if it were filled with sawdust.

Abruptly, the Bodachs surged toward them. Moira shrieked more in fury than in fear, and Rick found himself suddenly howling as he viciously swung the sword, causing a pair of Bodachs to stumble backward to avoid being cut in two. Out of the corner of his eye the boy saw Nion duck beneath the thrust of a spear and plunge his blade into a shriveled body. Faol knocked three attackers senseless with a violent blow of his shield, and ran another through with his spear. All about the boy were shouts and shrieks, the stamping of feet, the writhing of gray forms. A Bodach flung itself at him, clutching, and he noticed, absently, that its eyes shone red in the darkness.

And then, suddenly, another sound could be heard behind the noise of the yelling, shrieking Bodachs—a pure, sustained note that pierced through their uproar. It was the long, loud blast of a horn.

The Bodachs quickly fell back. Their shouts of rage became screams of terror. They flung aside their torches and weapons and fled in panic in all directions. Dozens of them went down before the silent rush of tall figures that had burst upon them from the rear.

In the next instant, a swarm of pale-haired men in silvery, metal-scale tunics surrounded the besieged group. Carrying spears that gleamed with wet blackness in the moonlight, they were shouting and laughing with Faol and Nion. Suddenly it dawned upon Moira that she and her companions had been saved.

"Rick, we're safe!" she exclaimed. "Praise be to the saints!"

With flushed face and shining eyes she peered about for her American cousin. She did not see him with Nion or Faol or standing among the tall Danaan warriors. She did not see him anywhere.

"Rick!" she called loudly, suddenly anxious.

There was no answer.

6

FAOL AND THE CAPTAIN OF THE BAND OF WARRIORS were talking in loud, gleeful voices. "In Danu's name, how came you to be here?" questioned Faol.

"We were encamped on the banks of the Grayflow at sunset," the other replied. "Then, word came from Lair Bhan to make haste to this place. And here we are, just in time it seems."

Moira scarcely heard them. Fear was squeezing her heart with an iron hand. Rick had been beside her when the Bodachs had made their attack, and she had seen him swing his sword at a pair of assailants before her attention had been diverted and she'd had to fend off an attacker herself. She hadn't seen him since then; what could have become of him? She peered again among the milling warriors, hoping she had merely missed seeing him the first time she had looked among them, then she began to move through the trampled grass, half fearing she might come across his crumpled body lying with a Bodach spear sticking out of it. Catching sight of the Luchorpan, she ran toward him. "Nion! I can't find Rick!"

"What?" The Luchorpan stared about, just as she had done. "Faol!" he shouted with such force that the cords stood out on his neck. "The boy is missing!"

At his shout the warriors stopped talking and laughing,

sensing that something was wrong. Faol, with dismay on his face, glanced quickly at Nion and the girl, then swung around and issued rapid orders. "Spread out and search! Look for a young, dark-haired lad of about twelve summers. He may have been injured in the fight, and if he is lying nearby somewhere, the grass will be hiding him from sight."

Swiftly and silently the men fanned out, moving intently through the moon-silvered grass that swished around their knees. Moira stood wringing her hands, her face twisted with worry. She knew that Rick wouldn't be lying down if he could stand and he wouldn't be silent if he could speak! Please, just let him be knocked out or something like that, thought Moira. Don't let him be badly hurt, or—or dead!

Minutes later the warriors began to drift back to where Faol stood with the Danaan captain, whose name was Alain. Most of the men reported with brief shakes of the head and terse words that they had found nothing. But one man came hurrying up, bearing a long sword. "I found this Danaan sword in a wide swath of trampled grass," he told Faol. "There had surely been a struggle, but there was no body and no blood."

"Aye, I gave this to him before the fight began," said Faol, taking the sword. He drew a deep breath. "Well, from what you say I would guess that he was overcome and carried off, leaving the sword behind."

"You mean the Bodachs have got him?" cried Moira. "What can we do?"

The Danaan captain, Alain, glanced at the sky. "I fear we can do nothing until dawn, *cailin,* and that is still some time away. But as soon as it is light we will see if we can pick up a trail and I will send a few searchers after him."

"You do not understand, Alain," Nion spoke up. "We

must get that boy back if it takes every man here to do it! The Bodachs were sent to capture him and the girl and deliver them to the Fomoiri. The Fomoiri want them for some purpose we cannot yet fathom, and if the boy falls into their hands it could be our undoing! We must try to regain him even if it means following his trail into the Shadow!"

The Danaan shook his head. "*You* do not understand, Nion. Things are in a delicate balance now. We dare not enter the Shadow until we are positive of victory, and even then it will take every warrior and wizard we can muster. To invade the northland with a war band this size would be folly. It is too small to accomplish anything and too large to escape detection."

"A small group, then," urged Nion. "Small enough to be undetected but large enough to be able to easily take the boy back from his captors. We *must* not let him fall into the hands of the Fomoiri!"

"Nion is right," seconded Faol. "I will go."

"I am with you," a sturdy, flame-bearded warrior called out. There were murmurs of assent from most of the others.

Alain gnawed his lip. "Very well, a small group," he agreed. He pointed to four of the men who had volunteered. "Faol will be your leader."

"I am going too," growled Nion.

"So am I!" declared Moira. She had quickly turned things over in her mind and had come to a decision. The thought of voluntarily putting herself in danger of capture by the Fomoiri was terrifying, but she felt she wouldn't be able to live with herself if she were safe somewhere while Rick was in danger. After all, he was her cousin, part of the family—to any Irishman, one of the most important considerations of all—and she simply could not desert him.

38

Besides, she couldn't bear the thought of being all by herself in this strange land with no link at all to her own world.

Nion and Faol looked at her with consternation. "Impossible!" the Luchorpan exploded. "'Twould be putting your head in a dragon's mouth, girl! We dare not risk having you captured as well as the boy!"

"This will be no simple thing, Moira," Faol warned. "Every step we take toward the north will be full of danger, and the Shadow, if we must enter it, is the heart of danger itself. The land beneath it is blighted, and abounds with monstrous things!"

"I don't care. I'm goin'!" Moira tilted her head back and stuck out her chin in the gesture of defiance Rick had noticed before the fight with the Bodachs. "I've *got* to go! I've got to help my cousin!"

"No!" Nion was equally firm. "You will go to Murias with Alain and his men. You'll be safe there."

"I won't!" The chin tilted higher. "They'll have to tie me up and carry me! And if I can get free I'll run away and try to find Rick. I'll run away from Murias itself if I have to!"

They stared at her. "I believe she would," said Faol at last, in a disapproving voice but with a suspicious quirk to his lips. He turned to Nion. "I think we must let her come with us, Nion. I have a feeling about this."

The Luchorpan flung up his hands. "Madness!" he shouted, and stalked away.

The quirk on Faol's lips had turned into a definite smile. "Very well then, *cailin,* come with us you shall. Now, there is some time until dawn, as Alain has said, so perhaps you should try to snatch what sleep you can." He unfastened his cloak and draped it around her. "I will awaken you at morning's first light."

☙ 7 ❧

I'VE GOT TO GET AWAY, Rick told himself. Somehow, I've got to get away! They'll take me to the Fomoiri!

It was morning, and he was in a tiny glade in the forest, sitting with his back against a tree trunk and his legs stretched out in front of him. His hands were free, but his legs were bound at the ankles with leather thongs, so knotted and twisted they probably couldn't have been untied by an escape artist from a circus act. His head throbbed painfully from the blow that had knocked him unconscious during the fight with the Bodachs; there was a tender lump above his temple that felt as big as a golf ball. His body ached, too, probably because he had spent most of the night slung over the shoulder of one of the grotesque creatures that had captured him as they hurried through the forest.

He stared with revulsion at his captors, who were busily engaged in something just a few steps away from him in the center of the glade. They were very different from each other. One of them was a Bodach; in daylight it was not quite as terrifying in appearance as it and the other Bodachs had seemed last night in the flickering red torchlight. Although the creature's hairless head and incredible scrawniness had made it and the others seem like ancient living mummies, Rick could see by its surprising strength and agility that it was probably fairly young. It was a three-foot-tall caricature of a human being, with an oversize head and abnormally long, thin arms and legs, which, coupled with the quick, scuttling movements it made, gave it a spiderlike quality.

The Bodach was bad enough in appearance, but at least it had a semblance of humanity. The other creature was completely monstrous. It was eight or nine feet tall, and its skin was the color of glistening, yellow butter. It wore no clothing, and except for the fact that it had arms, legs, and a round blob of a head, it was not at all humanlike. It resembled a thing that might have been made out of clay by a child. Its arms and legs were oddly malformed and seemed somehow to *curve* instead of bend at knee and elbow, as if the creature had no joints in its body. Worst of all, it had no face! Where eyes should have been there were merely two dark indentations, such as might have been made by someone pressing his thumbs into a soft substance. There was a slight ridge that might have been a nose, but Rick could see nothing that served as a mouth, and wondered absently how it was able to eat. The boy had spent most of the night across this thing's back, bouncing against its clammy, rubbery body as it jogged swiftly among the trees.

Rick stared at the two repulsive creatures, knowing that he was completely in their power and was almost certainly being taken to the menacing Fomoiri for some unknown purpose. He felt terror rising within himself. No! he thought desperately, knowing that he could lose control and become hysterical. He fought against the fear that threatened to engulf him, opening his mouth wide and taking in great gulps of air.

The Bodach heard the sounds and swiveled its head to

41

look at him. It studied him for a moment, then its mouth split into a ghastly travesty of a smile, showing rows of pointed teeth. It spoke in a mixture of thickly accented English and some other language, but Rick was able to get the general sense of what it was saying.

"Awake, *fear leanabh*?" The voice was a harsh croak. "*Maithe*! It is—*aimsir*—of eat." It came to his side in a single scuttling movement, digging into the large leather bag that hung over its shoulder and extending its hands to the boy with something in each of them. "*Aran, cais*," it said, grinning.

Rick accepted the objects with hesitation, then saw with growing enthusiasm that one was a slab of coarse brown bread and the other a chunk of strong-smelling, yellowish cheese. He suddenly realized he was ravenously hungry, and he began to wolf down the food.

"*Maithe, maithe*!" The Bodach rocked on its heels and slapped its hands together gleefully as it watched him eat. Rick wondered why it was bothering to feed him; it certainly didn't have the look or manner of a kindly sort of creature. He decided the Fomoiri must want him in good condition for some reason and had probably told the Bodachs to treat him and Moira gently if they were captured. Yet he was sure the Fomoiri were not kindly creatures either, and if they wanted him well fed and in good condition, he suspected there was a sinister purpose behind it!

When he had finished the bread and cheese the Bodach gestured toward the center of the glade. "*Uisge*?" it said, questioningly.

He saw that there was a tiny pool, or perhaps a well, surrounded by a rim of rocks, where the Bodach was pointing. The word it had said, which had sounded like

42

"ooishkay," must mean "water" or "drink," he thought, and licking his dry lips he nodded vigorously. The Bodach took him by the shoulders, and despite its small size and scrawniness it easily dragged him to the edge of the well. Resting his hands on the rocks, the boy lowered his head and gulped cool water into his throat.

Something was pressing painfully against his left hand. Still gulping water, he let his fingers judge it. It was a sharp-edged stone, jutting out of the ring of stones around the pool. And it was loose.

An idea flashed into Rick's mind. Carefully, he worked the stone out of place and let it drop into his hand. Closing his fingers around it, he raised his head from the surface of the water and struggled to a kneeling position, sliding the stone into the pocket of his jeans as he did so. He glanced around guiltily, to see if he had been observed, but the yellow thing's back was to him, and the Bodach, squatting behind him, was busily examining the contents of its shoulder bag. As if aware of his eyes on it, it looked up at him. He felt that some expression on his face or in his eyes might make it suspicious, and to divert its attention and cover up his fear that it might somehow discover he had the stone, he spoke to it.

"Where are you taking me?"

A furrow of puzzlement appeared between its eyes.

"Where are we going?" asked Rick slowly, raising his eyebrows questioningly and using his hands to indicate the three of them and then motion in several directions.

The Bodach apparently grasped his meaning. It stretched out a skinny arm and gestured northward. "*Tuath*," it said. "Fomor."

Well, that's what I figured, thought Rick. "What will the

Fomoiri"—he pointed toward the north—"do to me?" On the last word he touched himself.

The skull-like face broke into its horrible grin. A stone-bladed knife suddenly appeared in the Bodach's hand, and the creature leaned forward, placing the weapon's point against Rick's throat. The boy stiffened in terror, but the Bodach was apparently just demonstrating, to make him understand. *"Fuil ruadh!"* it said gleefully. *"Fuil ruadh—an aon óg!* For—*Cean Cruach!"*

Rick paled. The Bodach's meaning seemed clear. Its action in putting the knife at his throat surely meant that the Fomoiri were going to cut his throat, and the word "rooa," which it had spoken, sounded like one of the Gaelic words Moira had taught him: the word meaning "red"—the color of blood! Apparently the Fomoiri were going to kill him and give his blood to someone or something called Kahn Kroog. He was going to be sacrificed! He shuddered violently, and the Bodach, which had been watching him in anticipation, screeched with laughter.

Then, all at once, it became businesslike. Springing to its feet, it rattled out a string of words at the silent yellow creature, which rose with a sinuous uncoiling motion and reached for Rick. The boy felt himself being effortlessly picked up and in a moment was hanging head down over the yellow back, like a sack of potatoes.

The creature moved along at a steady trot, loping in and out among the trees without a break in stride, as smoothly as a machine. The little Bodach moved along ahead of it just as easily, its spindly legs pumping up and down like pistons. For what must have been nearly an hour, the boy watched the carpet of gold and copper-colored leaves flow past be-

44

neath him until, lulled by the monotonous motion, he fell asleep.

He was awakened by the thump of his body against the ground and glanced about with half-closed eyes. They were in another glade, and from the slant of the sunlight filtering through the overhead canopy of leaves, it was now about midafternoon. The Bodach glanced at the boy for a moment, then, satisfied that he was still completely helpless, dropped to the ground, rolled onto its side, and closed its eyes. The yellow creature stretched out flat on its stomach, its body seeming to settle into the ground.

Well, they had been running most of the night, had stopped for only a short time this morning, had run most of the rest of the day, and had now obviously stopped to sleep for a time, thought Rick. He fought to control his breathing; in his sudden excitement his chest had begun to rise and fall rapidly and he feared one of the creatures might notice. This was his chance, and he intended to take it, come what may! If what the Bodach had told him was true, it meant certain death to let himself be taken to the Fomoiri. He would try to escape and take his chances in the forest.

He could scarcely believe his good fortune in having only his legs tied. Apparently his captors were completely confident that he wouldn't be able to untie himself, and he had to admit that he probably wouldn't have been able to—but he had the sharp stone and his hands were free to use it! It had been stupid of the two creatures not to tie his hands, but they didn't seem very bright; indeed, the yellow thing was little more than an animal. At any rate, he was going to take advantage of his luck. Maybe my lucky stone is working, he thought almost jovially.

45

He waited patiently until the Bodach began to snore. The other thing lay absolutely motionless, apparently not even breathing! Carefully, Rick slid the sharp stone out of his pocket. Easing himself slowly to a sitting position, he leaned forward and began to saw at the thongs that bound his legs.

It was hard work, and he was soon clenching his teeth to keep from panting. A thong parted and he attacked another one. Once, he froze in fear as the Bodach stirred and grunted, as if coming awake. But its snores resumed and Rick set to work again, praying that neither creature would awaken and catch him. They would then tie his hands for sure, and his only chance to escape would be lost.

Another thong parted. He wiggled his ankles and worried the bindings with his hands. Abruptly, one of his feet was loose! In seconds, so was the other.

Gently, oh so gently, he got to his knees. It felt as if pins and needles were piercing his legs and feet as the partially stopped blood circulation in his legs resumed full flow. Forcing himself to ignore the discomfort, Rick stood up, fixing his eyes on the two sleeping creatures.

He took a step away, then another, moving in the direction opposite to the one they had been following, placing his feet carefully on patches of moss and dirt so as not to make any rustling sounds in the litter of dry leaves. His breath was coming in whispered pants, and his stomach ached with fear. Please let me make it, he thought. Please!

Half a dozen steps, then a dozen. The glade was now lost from sight among the trees. He increased his pace. Panic welled up within him; I've got to move faster, he thought, I've got to! They could still catch me if they woke up now!

He began to run, completely heedless of the noise his feet

made. He dodged among the trees, hurdled a fallen trunk, twisted under low branches. He ran until he was gasping with the taste of blood in his breath. Then, gloriously, just as he came to a kind of grassy avenue that stretched between curving rows of trees on each side, he got his second wind. He sped on with greater freedom of movement, every stride leaving his captors farther behind. I'm free, his heart sang, I got away! He knew the feeling of the mouse that has just eluded the swiping claws of a cat. He was lost in a vast, unknown forest, but at least he now had a chance. Death lay behind him, and whatever lay ahead could be no worse.

❧ 8 ❧

A HAND WAS GENTLY SHAKING MOIRA'S SHOULDER. "Yes, Mum, I'm awake," she murmured dutifully. Then, the recollection of where she was and what had happened came flooding into her mind. Her eyes shot open and she saw Faol stooping over her, his form silhouetted against a dark sky into which pale gray light was slowly seeping.

"It is dawn, *cailin*," he said. "We must make ready."

Moira thrust sleep away and scrambled to her feet, conscious of an uncomfortable twinge of worry and excitement prodding her stomach. She ran her fingers through her tangled hair, feeling distinctly grubby after a night spent sleeping on the ground, and licked her lips, wishing she could brush her teeth somehow.

Her distaste for her condition was apparent, and Faol smiled faintly. "I am afraid there is no way for you to cleanse yourself in your usual manner," he told her, "but you must get used to such inconvenience. We will have to live in this fashion while we are seeking the lad."

"It doesn't matter," Moira assured him. "Finding Rick is what's important!"

While the sky continued to lighten, she shared a quick breakfast of dry oatcakes and sips of water from a leather flask with Faol and Nion. They had spent the night among

48

the warriors of the Danaan war band, and now two of the warriors who were to accompany them in search of Rick came and squatted at Faol's side.

"We have found what seems to be the track, leading into the forest," one of the men announced. "Two sets of footprints—a Bodach and a Brollachan, traveling together. A Bodach would not travel with a Boneless One unless he had some use for it, and we think it may be carrying the boy for him."

"They were heading north," the second man added, "as they would be if they were taking the lad to the abode of the Fomoiri."

Faol jerked his head in a single nod. "I think this is indeed the track we should follow." He stood up, and Nion and Moira scrambled to do likewise.

Alain, the Danaan captain, strode toward them. "Are you ready to leave?" he asked, and Faol nodded. "Then the fortune of Dagda go with you. I shall withdraw this war band to the east bank of the Grayflow and send a messenger to the High King, telling him of this pursuit of yours." He clapped Faol on the shoulder, shook Nion's hand, and bowed to Moira with his hand over his heart. Then he turned away and rejoined his men, who were forming up to march.

Faol stooped and picked up his spear and shield from the ground. The other two warriors who were part of the search party had joined the first pair, and the four of them stood waiting. "Let us go," said Faol.

With two of the Danaan preceding them and two following, Moira, Nion, and Faol entered the forest. In the brightening dawn it seemed even more sparkling and jewel-like than it had been at late afternoon the day before, but Moira took little notice of its beauty. Her mind was a jumble of thoughts—worry about her cousin, concern over the anguish her parents must be feeling at her disappearance, and uneasiness about the dangers of this journey she had determined to make.

The party moved through the trees at a quick, steady pace, following a spoor that was completely invisible to Moira but that was apparently as clear as a picture to the two Danaan trackers, Teine and Foghar, who were leading the way. The girl was greatly encouraged by their obvious skill and confidence.

Shortly before noon they reached the glade of the little pool where Rick had been fed by the Bodach. The two Danaan scouts examined the area, noting the patterns of crushed grass and the cluster of ants that swarmed about some crumbs of bread and cheese beneath a tree.

"There is no doubt this is the right track," the red-bearded Teine told Faol. "Two sets of footprints, those of the Bodach and Brollachan lead into this glade, but *three* forms reclined on the grass here, and one was bigger than the Bodach but far smaller than the Boneless One. It could only have been the boy." He pointed at a tree on the edge of the glade. "He sat beneath that tree, and it appears that they fed him."

Faol's eyes gleamed with satisfaction. "Surely, we must be no more than half a day behind them, for they started out near midnight and we followed at early dawn. They cannot know that we are following them, so sooner or later they will stop to sleep, and if the fortune of Dagda is with us, we shall come upon them then! Let us hurry!"

They continued on through the forest. Their midday meal, again consisting of only oatcakes and sips of water, they ate as they walked. Moira now felt sure that they would find and rescue her cousin this very day, but she was somewhat worried about how the two creatures that held the boy captive might be treating him.

"Do you think Rick is all right?" she asked Faol. "Do you think those two things might hurt him?"

Faol shook his head vigorously to reassure her. "Teine said there were clear signs that they had given Rick food, and that shows he is being well treated. Bodachs are spiteful things and often do torture prisoners, but I suspect that the Bodach that has Rick is following orders from the Fomoiri to bring any captive to them in good condition, and he would not dare to disobey his masters."

"I just wish I knew why the Fomoiri want Rick at all," Moira said. "I just don't understand it."

"We still cannot be sure it *is* Rick they want," said Nion, from behind her. "The Bodach may have taken him simply because it was able to. For that matter, we cannot be sure this is not just a means of luring *you* into their hands—which is why I wish you would stop right here and let me take you to Murias!"

Moira sighed and shook her head. "I can't do that, Nion. I've *got* to help find Rick, even though it puts me in danger. Can't you understand?"

"I can," said Faol gently. "I have seen warriors risk sure death to save a comrade."

They tramped on as the beams of sunlight that reached through gaps in the leaves slowly turned from golden to orange. And finally, near sunset, they came to the second glade, where the Bodach and Brollachan had lain down to sleep and Rick had made his escape.

The Danaan trackers, Teine and Foghar, studied the place with growing puzzlement. Teine paced about staring

51

at the ground, went a short distance into the woods and looked about there, then returned to where the others waited.

"Something happened here that I do not understand," he confessed. "The grass in the glade is all trampled down by the small feet of the Bodach, as if it were dancing or jumping about in rage. Then, it appears as if the Bodach and Brollachan split up and went in two different directions, which puzzles me greatly."

"Which way should we go, then?" Faol asked anxiously.

The red-bearded Danaan hesitated, squatting on his heels and peering off among the trees. "The Brollachan headed north, the same direction they have been going all along," he said at last. "Only it could have carried the boy, the Bodach is too small. I do not know why the Bodach left, but I think the Brollachan must still have the lad and is taking him to Fomor by itself."

"Then we must follow the Boneless One," said Faol. Teine nodded and rose to his feet. In dejected silence, for they had hoped to rescue Rick from his captors by now, Moira, Nion, Faol, and the four Danaan warriors moved out of the glade.

From a perch high in a tree some distance back in the forest, the Bodach watched them go, fingering the leather thongs with which Rick had been tied, and which, had they been left in the glade, would have told Teine and Foghar that the boy had escaped. When the Bodach had awakened to find the cut thongs lying in the grass and the boy gone, it had flown into a wild rage, stamping the ground and flailing the stolid Brollachan with the thongs. Then it had darted into the forest in hope of finding Rick or his trail. Left by itself, the dull-witted Brollachan, which had been carefully implanted with the idea that it must head north, had started out in that direction once again.

The Bodach had prowled about for a time, seeking Rick's tracks, but it was not the tracker that Teine or Foghar was, and it could not detect which way the boy had gone. While searching, it had heard the Danaan approaching and had climbed the tree to hide.

Now it came scrambling down and stood for a while, wondering what to do. It had hoped to gain great favor from the Fomoiri by bringing them one of the two young humans they sought, which it had managed to knock unconscious and had given to the Brollachan to carry just before the Danaan war band had arrived to put the other Bodachs to flight. Now it knew it could expect only anger from the Fomoiri for having lost the young human—and the thought of Fomoiri anger made the Bodach cringe in terror.

Cursing the boy, the Fomoiri, and the Danaan alike, the scrawny creature turned finally and hurried off among the trees, seeking some lonely place where it could safely hide from the wrath of the Fomoiri or the angry vengeance of the Danaan, depending upon whichever might prevail in the titanic battle to decide the mastery of the Middle Kingdom, a battle that, as it knew, would soon take place.

9

MOIRA, NION, AND THE FIVE DANAAN moved in silence, as the forest shadows deepened from dusk into darkness. When the track of the Brollachan could no longer be seen, Faol called a halt. They all shared a supper that, like breakfast and lunch, consisted merely of oatcakes and water. A tiny, carefully tended fire glowed dimly.

"At another time, and in another part of the forest, we might have had a haunch of deer or a brace of rabbits, roasted over a big cheery fire," remarked Faol to Moira. "But we dare not risk a bright fire here. We are too near the Shadow, and such things might be noticed."

"It's no matter," Moira assured him absently, her eyes gazing into the blackness of the woods in the direction they were headed. Then she swiveled her gaze to him. "Faol—do you think we have a chance to catch up to them?"

"I cannot truly say, Moira," he answered after a moment. "Teine and Foghar felt that the Brollachan had left the glade only a short time before we arrived there, and that we were close behind it. But it had probably been sleeping, and now it may travel all night, while we cannot follow until there is enough light to see by."

Teine, seated beside Faol, leaned forward toward the girl. "But do not give up hope, *cailin*. A Brollachan has little wit, and without the Bodach to prod it along, it will have no thought that it is being followed and will likely move more slowly. I feel that we have a good chance to catch up with it soon—perhaps as soon as midday tomorrow."

"By midday tomorrow," remarked Nion grimly, "we shall be within the Shadow!"

"Well, we knew it might come to that," Faol reminded him. "But if Teine is right, we will still be close enough to the edge of the Shadow so that we may be able to regain the lad and get back out again before the Fomoiri even become aware of us."

Nion sighed deeply. "I pray to every god and spirit there is that you are right," he said, his eyes resting upon Moira.

They slept, Nion and each of the Danaan taking turns as sentry during the night. When it was barely light enough to see, the sentry on watch awakened the rest of them and they hastened on their way again. Moira noticed that the trees were becoming more widely spaced, and by the time the sun was fully into the sky the search party had reached the edge of the forest, looking out upon a vast meadowland.

Moira quickly became aware of an incredible sight. The meadow was painted gold by the bright sun overhead, but the sunlight did not fill the entire sky as usual—instead, a dark gray curtain stretched across the distant horizon as far as the eye could see, and extended straight up into a sky as dark as night. It was as if the world of the Middle Kingdom was divided exactly in half, with one half in daylight and the other in darkness!

"Is that—the Shadow?" asked Moira, in a near whisper.

Nion answered, "Aye. The Shadow of Fomor."

"The trail is fresh and clear here," observed Foghar, pointing to the ground. The grass of the meadow was knee high to the tall Danaan warriors, and an obvious swath of broken, bent, and flattened stalks began at the edge of the meadow and led into it, made by the big feet of the Brollachan. "From the look of it, he is plodding, not running," said Foghar. "He cannot be very far ahead."

"Come!" said Faol. At a half trot they began to move through the meadow, Faol in the lead, easily following the clear track. Moira was right behind him, peering eagerly ahead, hoping to catch sight of the creature that she thought was carrying Rick toward the great blot of darkness in the distance.

They moved steadily through the meadow until noontime, alternately jogging and walking. The pall of darkness ahead grew ever nearer, and by the time the sun was straight overhead in the daylight portion of the sky, the darkness loomed over the seven travelers like a vast wall, only steps away. Within it, the land seemed gray and indistinct.

"Hold!" called Nion, and the others stopped at his shout, looking at him.

"What is it?" asked Faol.

Nion looked at Moira. "One last time I beg you, Moira, not to enter into the Shadow," he said. "If it is you alone the Fomoiri seek, or if it is you and Rick together that they need, you are going straight into their hands and perhaps assuring them of victory! Go back to the edge of the forest with Faol, or me, or one of the others and wait there until the rest of the band either returns with Rick or fails to come out by sunset. But do not go into the Shadow yourself!"

Moira looked back at the Luchorpan without speaking right away, as if she were gathering her thoughts for what to say. "Nion, I don't want to go in there," she said finally.

"I'm scared—the saints *know* I'm scared! But I *must* go. It isn't even just because I want to help find Rick. I feel I must go into the Shadow because—there's something I have to do in there!"

Nion stared at her in silence. After a few moments Faol spoke. "Very well, then, we shall all go on. But listen to me now, Moira and Nion. If we are attacked in there, you must try to get away. Do not try to help us; we five Danaan will sell our lives dearly to enable you to escape. Nion, you must see that she gets safely to Murias." He looked sharply at the girl. "Do you promise, Moira—at the first sign of danger you must flee with Nion!"

She nodded. "I promise."

"Come, then," said Faol, and walked into the darkness.

Passing into it, each person went instantly from high noon to evening dusk. But the Shadow was more than just a covering of darkness, they quickly found. The grass that was tall, green, and gold in the meadow on the other side of the darkness was short, gray, and brittle here, and nearby trees were stunted and leafless. The Shadow was like a fog that made everything blurry and indistinct, reducing vision to no more than a few hundred yards on all sides. There was a chill in the air, like that of an evening in early winter, which made them hunch their shoulders for warmth.

Nion spat. "The foulness of Fomor," he growled. "This is what they would do to the whole of the Middle Kingdom— turn it into a place of gray sadness!"

Faol was peering about intently. "I think it best if we do not talk much," he counseled in a low voice. "This place stinks to me of evil sorcery and unclean things. Let us not call attention to ourselves."

The Danaan warriors had taken up a kind of diamond-shaped formation around Moira and Nion. Teine and Foghar were about a dozen yards ahead, a warrior walked on each side, and Faol brought up the rear. In complete silence, they moved rapidly through the menacing grayness, following the track of the Brollachan, which was actually easier to see here as a trail of broad, flattened splotches through the brittle, gray grass.

Moira could not keep from looking about apprehensively, but she saw no sign of life, only the bleak, gray landscape, which grew depressingly monotonous as they tramped through it. After a time, it seemed to the girl as if they had been walking for hours, and that it must be nearly nighttime, but the dusky darkness of the Shadow was unchanged. Perhaps there was neither day nor night here, she thought. Perhaps there was only the eternal, never-ending twilight.

Gradually, the landscape began to change. A few trees appeared, and then more, thicker and closer together, until the travelers were moving through a sparse forest that seemed to be made up mostly of leafless willow trees, their long, slender branches trailing down like the coarse hair of giants. The ground underfoot was damp and squishy, and there was an odor in the air as of something long dead.

They passed through the woods and came out onto another broad meadowland, but the grass here was nearly knee high and writhed snakily in a chill wind, so that the ground seemed to be rippling.

"Look!" said Foghar suddenly, pointing. "There he is!"

Her heart beginning to pound with hope and excitement, Moira peered through the dusky haze toward where Foghar pointed. She could barely make out a tiny moving patch, far in the distance.

"Spread out," ordered Faol in a low voice. "We must try to surround him. Run!"

In a single long line they pelted through the waving grass, closing toward the distant, plodding Brollachan, which remained unaware of them. Gradually, they were near enough to be able to see the creature clearly.

"Mórrígan's curse!" Faol exploded, coming to an instant stop. "It doesn't have the lad!"

Moira let out a wail of disappointment. It was true, the Brollachan was alone! It did not have Rick! Stopping abruptly, she stared in a turmoil of confusion and consternation at the ungainly yellow creature. Where *was* her cousin? Did the Fomoiri have him? Was he *dead*? Would she ever see him again? Realizing that she had failed in her resolution to rescue the boy, for whom she felt responsible, she burst into tears.

Hearing the sounds behind it, the Brollachan, now only a hundred yards or so ahead, turned and for the first time saw its pursuers. It regarded them for a few moments with its eyeless face, then broke into a shambling run.

Ignoring it, the Danaan came together, crowding around the sobbing girl. Teine was tugging at his red beard, his forehead wrinkled in thought. His eyes lit up.

"Hold, *cailin*, don't grieve," he said. "The lad is safe! At least, that is, the Fomoiri do not have him. I understand, now, what happened in that glade where the Bodach and Brollachan split up. *The lad escaped!* The Bodach went after him and the Brollachan went off on its own."

"Of course!" Faol exclaimed. "Come, let's get out of this *liath marbh* place and back to the great forest. We'll either find the lad, or if the Bodach has found him we'll be able to head it off before it can bring him here!"

As one, they turned to go back the way they had come. But as they did, the clumps of tall, gray, swirling grass in which they stood whipped in toward them, twisting around their feet and legs. Warriors, Luchorpan, and girl found themselves suddenly bound to the earth, unable to move.

"*Latha dubh!*" cursed Nion. "Enchantment!" With his short sword he attempted to hack through the gray strands that held him, but it was useless, like trying to cut through steel wires. The Danaan warriors struggled to tear the clutching stuff away from themselves.

"Look!" Moira gave a horrified shriek. Racing toward them out of the gloom came a score of big, black shapes— wolflike animals the size of horses, with blazing red eyes and savagely sharp teeth. Mounted upon them were shining-eyed, white-faced Fomoiri in scaly black armor. One of these gestured at the ensnared people, and called out something in a deep, throaty voice.

"Do as he says," said Faol bitterly, and tossed his spear to the ground. "We are helpless, the *púcas* will tear us to pieces if we do not obey!" The other warriors and Nion dropped their weapons, their faces grim.

The wolflike *púcas* formed a ring around the captives. One of the Fomoiri swung himself off his mount's back. Ignoring the Danaan and the Luchorpan, he moved straight toward Moira, who gave a little sob of fear.

Halting at arm's length, the creature scrutinized the girl, who stared back, wide-eyed. The Fomor's white face was as smooth as polished marble, completely clear of any of the lines, wrinkles, or textures of human skin. Its eyes were pools of glinting silver, without white or pupil.

The Fomor stretched its arm toward Moira, who flinched. Then, abruptly, the creature jerked its hand back,

60

making an angry hissing sound as it did. It stared at the girl a moment more, then turned away and spoke, in a language that snarled and hissed, to the other Fomoiri, who began to dismount and move toward the captives.

Over the head of each Danaan and Nion was cast a slender loop of some shiny substance. Immediately, each man and the Luchorpan felt a terrible coldness seeping into his body, and his limbs became so sluggish he could barely move. The gray tendrils of grass that had held them fast loosened and fell away from their feet, and each captive was tossed over the back of a *púca,* to hang with head down on one side and feet dangling on the other, while the riders mounted behind them.

The leader reached down, slipped his hands under Moira's armpits, and lifted her onto his *púca's* back, in front of him. Instantly, without command, the wolflike steeds were on the move, running with incredible speed back toward the distant gloom out of which they had appeared, carrying Moira and her helpless companions to an unknown fate.

High overhead, a pair of bright, keen eyes watched them go. An eagle soared in the darkened sky, slowly moving in broad circles as it observed what took place below. Had any of the Fomoiri chanced to look up and see it they might have been curious, for eagles are birds of daytime and sunlight, not of twilight, and they are hunters of rabbits and other small animals, of which there were none within the Shadow. The presence of the bird was most unusual.

Turning in a graceful curve, the eagle began to beat its wings vigorously, driving itself through the air toward the land that lay in sunlight beyond the Shadow, moving with great speed, as if it had some vital purpose to fulfill.

❧10❧

AFTER WANDERING IN THE FOREST for twenty-four hours, Rick was not quite as confident as he had been when he made his escape.

The night was particularly bad. At sunset he scrambled up into the branches of a gnarly oak and found a perch some twenty feet above the ground; he felt it would not be wise to spend the hours of darkness on the forest floor. Worried that he might turn in his sleep and fall to the ground, he strapped one leg to a branch with his belt. But he slept very little, for the night was full of crackles and whispers and patterings that he found most unnerving, and that made him glad he had taken to the tree.

As the forest became visible in the first red flush of dawn, the boy climbed down and set off on his way, stiff and bleary-eyed. Another worry now occupied him—he needed water. He knew that a person could go for quite a long time without food, but how long could someone stay alive without water? Not very long, he feared. He wandered about for several hours, and was becoming desperately thirsty when luck led him to the edge of a narrow gully. There, moving below, was a small, clear stream. Scrambling down the slope, he threw himself onto the ground at the edge of the stream and lowered his head to the water, gulping eagerly.

His thirst relieved, Rick squatted on his haunches beside the stream and considered his predicament. He had no idea of which way to go, so one way seemed as good as another as long as he didn't head back in the direction from which he had come, for that might lead him back into the clutches of the Bodach and Brollachan, whom he supposed were hunting for him. Inasmuch as water was obviously a necessity, he decided to stay near this water he had just found by simply following the stream. But which way? He knew, of course, that rivers flow from high ground down to a lake or sea, and he suddenly remembered that the stronghold of the Fomoiri was in some northern sea, on an island, so it seemed wisest to follow the water upstream in the opposite direction toward high ground. Rising to his feet he squared his shoulders and set out.

Water was certainly no longer a problem, but it wasn't long before Rick began to dwell on food. He had eaten nothing since the bit of bread and cheese that the Bodach had given him yesterday morning, and his stomach was complaining. He began to look about for nuts or berries, for he felt sure, from things he had read, that a forest must be full of various kinds of nut trees and fruit bushes. Then he realized that nuts and most kinds of berries were the produce of autumn, and it was now only early summer. No nuts or berries yet.

What could he eat then? Leaves? He stripped a handful of leaves from a low-hanging branch, stared at them doubtfully, then stuffed them into his mouth and began to chew. After a moment he spat out the wad of green and made a face. No help there!

A cluster of pallid mushrooms peeping out of the dead leaves underfoot caught his eye. He hesitated for a moment, considering them, then went resolutely on. He knew that many kinds of mushrooms were highly poisonous, but he couldn't tell one kind from another and might be risking a painful death if he ate something he wasn't sure of.

Soon he could think of nothing but food. Hamburgers and french fries! Pizza! He groaned faintly. The brown tufts of the cattails that grew in profusion along the stream made him think of plump sausages. He groaned again.

Plodding along with his hands pressed to his stomach, he suddenly became aware of a strong desire to turn away from the stream and move at a right angle from it into the forest. Before he was even conscious of doing so, he had clambered up the sloping side of the gully and was walking away from the water. Puzzled, he stopped abruptly. Why am I doing this, he thought. I wanted to stay near the stream, so I'd be sure of having water. Why am I going away from it? But the feeling that this was the right way to go was so strong that after a few moments he continued on. It was almost as if someone were calling to him.

He had probably traveled a good mile into the forest when, walking through a tight cluster of trees, he stopped in panic. He had come into another small glade, and on the silvery trunk of a dead tree that lay in the center of the glade was seated a man. His hands were folded on his lap and his head was down, but the instant Rick came through the trees, the man looked up at him.

Rick's first inclination was to turn and run. The man certainly wasn't a Fomor, but he didn't seem like a Danaan, either. He wore a loose, golden-orange robe, and his head was bare. Red hair fell to his shoulders, but his face was clean-shaven. He seemed young. A big bird, a hawk or perhaps an eagle, was perched on his shoulder, looking at Rick with fierce, intelligent-seeming eyes.

64

"Ah, you are here," said the man in a pleasant voice, his face breaking into a smile. "Be not afraid, Rick, I am no servant of the Fomoiri. I am known as Lair Bhan, and I am High Druid of the Danaan. And this is Neamh Suil." He indicated the bird. Then he patted the log. "Come sit down and let us talk."

Baffled, Rick moved forward and seated himself on the log beside the man. "You know me?"

Lair Bhan looked into Rick's eyes. His own eyes were calm and wise. "Better than you are aware. I watched over you and the maiden, Moira, while the Fomoiri were seeking you in your own world, and kept them from you as long as I was able. And when they would have seized you on the *sidhe*, it was I who brought you here and had the Luchorpan on hand to look after you. I thought you would be safe then, so I turned my attention to other matters, and later, when I learned that the Bodachs were hunting you, I could do no more than send word to Alain's war band to go to your aid. And when I was finally able to look to you and Moira again, I found that you had been captured—and escaped." He smiled and clapped Rick on the shoulder. "That was well done!" He regarded the boy thoughtfully. "But I suspect you have had nothing much to eat for some time. You must be starving!" He indicated a leathern bag at his feet. "Here is food. Help yourself to as much as you want."

"Thanks!" Rick dived at the bag, eagerly spread it open, and found that it contained several small loaves of bread, a big slab of hard cheese, and a large quantity of stiff, brownish strips that he suspected were some kind of dried or smoked meat. He attacked the food, alternating bites of bread with chews of the dried meat. He ate so fast he hardly had time to taste the food, yet it seemed to be the most delicious meal he had ever eaten. It's probably because I'm so hungry, he thought. I guess I *was* nearly starving!

"Here is water," said Lair Bhan, pointing at another leathern bag, equipped with a stoppered neck, that hung by a strap from a broken branch on the log.

Mouth full, Rick nodded his thanks. Suddenly, he was struck by a thought. He swallowed hastily and spoke. "You've been *waiting* here for me, haven't you? How did you know I'd come here?"

"I called you to this place, with what is known as a summoning spell," the man answered. "I hope you don't mind. It was easier and much quicker than to find you by hunting through the forest, although I had a general idea of where you were."

Rick stared at the man, his mind working even as he continued to chew furiously. There was an aura of knowledge and power about Lair Bhan. He had said that he was a "High Druid," and the boy remembered reading that the men known as Druids in his world were supposed to have been magicians. Certainly, what this man claimed to have done was magical—to have plucked Rick and Moira out of their world and brought them here, and to have caused Rick to make his way unerringly through the woods to this spot. It seemed to Rick that Lair Bhan surely must know a great deal more about the things that were going on in this world than Nion, or Faol, or certainly the Bodach, who were the only others the boy had talked with.

"If you know about all this stuff," he said, "do *you* know why the Fomoiri are after Moira and me? The Bodach told me they wanted to sacrifice me to somebody named Kahn Kroog, or something like that. Is that why they want us? Will killing us help them somehow?"

66

"The Bodach was lying to you, Rick," Lair Bhan told him. "They delight in cruelty, and it would have happily tortured you if it dared, but the Fomoiri had ordered that you be brought to them unharmed, so it tortured you the only way it could, by trying to frighten and worry you." He shook his head. "No, the Fomoiri have been seeking to capture both you and Moira alive, so that they could examine you and determine which of you was the one they had to fear. And they have now learned that it was not Moira. It is you."

Rick was silent for a time. "I sure can't figure it out!" he burst forth finally. "There's nothing special about me! I'm just an ordinary kid. I haven't got any magic or superpower, or anything like that!"

The man's gray eyes regarded him. "There *is* a power within you, Rick. It reveals itself a little, so that I can sense it, but it is deeply hidden and I cannot tell what it is or what form it takes."

"Well, why didn't the Fomoiri just try to kill Moira and me, then?" wondered the boy. "That would have solved all their problems, wouldn't it?"

"Not at all. Death does not necessarily eliminate power, quite often it *releases* it, with drastic results. The Fomoiri would not dare kill you until they could determine whether the power was truly dangerous to them, and how they could nullify it. That was why they have been seeking you."

Rick took a deep breath. "Well, they didn't get me!" He stared at the ground for a moment, then looked back up at the Druid. "Can you help me get to Murias, where they're taking Moira? Man, I bet she's worried sick about me!"

Now it was Lair Bhan who took a deep breath and let it out in a heavy sigh. "Now comes the part of our talk I have been dreading," he said. "I must tell you, Rick, that Moira is not safely in Murias. She, Faol, the Luchorpan, and some warriors set out to follow your captors in hopes of saving you. They could not tell that you had escaped, and they followed the trail of the Brollachan on into the Shadow of Fomor, thinking that the Brollachan must still be carrying you." He looked straight into the boy's eyes and placed a hand on his shoulder. "They have been taken captive by the Fomoiri."

Rick gasped. "No! Are you sure? How do you know?"

Lair Bhan reached up to stroke the feathers of the eagle on his shoulder. "Only a short time before you answered my summoning spell, Neamh Suil brought me word of their capture, which he himself witnessed. His name means 'sky eye,' and he is my source for seeing things that take place far from where I am."

"Well, can you do something? Can you save them?"

The Druid stood up abruptly, startling the eagle so that it spread its wings and hunched its head. The man soothed it, stroking it again with his hand. "I can do nothing now. They are within the very heart of the Shadow, in the firm grasp of Fomor. But—"

He began to pace back and forth. "Listen to me, lad. The things that have been stirring here in the Middle Kingdom are moving swiftly toward a conclusion. Even at this moment, the entire war host of the Danaan is marching toward the Shadow, for the High King fears that if you and Moira fall into the hands of the Fomoiri they may be able to use you somehow against the Danaan. Consequently, he has decided that the final battle against Fomor must take place now, before the Fomoiri can grow any stronger."

Rick's eyes widened with hope. "Then—then *they'll* save Moira and the others."

"No," said the man, his back to Rick. "They cannot." He

68

turned to face the boy. "It is within my power to see that which the future may hold. Most of what lies ahead is dim and uncertain, but one thing is very clear—the power that the Fomoiri can muster now is greater than that of the Danaan, even with the help of myself and the other Druids. As things now stand, the Danaan will be beaten."

Rick considered the implications of the man's words. "But what will happen, then?" he asked in a stricken voice.

"What could happen is that your cousin and friends may be killed, or at best they will be enslaved along with the rest of the dwellers in the Middle Kingdom," answered Lair Bhan, "including myself and you. And before long, the power of Fomor will once again creep into your world to cause untold misery there!"

He took a step forward, looking down at the boy. "But there is one flicker of hope in this darkness. The future is not *set*, it can be altered, although with great effort. And there is something the Fomoiri fear, and if they fear it, it may be the thing that could alter the future and bring their downfall. If it can be brought onto the side of the Danaan in the final battle, it might turn the tide."

He knelt, bringing his eyes level with the worried eyes of the boy. "Rick, it is *you* the Fomoiri fear! It is that hidden power of yours. I believe that you are the only hope of the Danaan, the Middle Kingdom, and your world as well. And so I ask you: Will you come with me now, into the Shadow, into the very heart of the danger that has threatened you, on the slim chance that whatever it is that is within you will come forth and save us all from the Shadow of Fomor?"

❧11❧

RICK'S FIRST REACTION TO LAIR BHAN'S WORDS was near
shock. The thought of deliberately taking himself straight
into the hands of those terrifying, icy-eyed creatures who
had been trying to get hold of him for the last few days put
him on the edge of panic. No, he couldn't do it!

But you've got to, a voice seemed to whisper within him.
You're the only hope for all the good people of this world, the
people like Nion, and Faol, and Lair Bhan. You may be the
only hope for the people of *your* world, too—and that in-
cludes your mom and dad and all your relatives and friends.
And don't forget Moira—you're her only hope, and she's in
trouble because she was trying to help *you*. Shouldn't you
try to help her now?

Yes, he decided, he certainly should. He should do this
for her sake, even if for no other, but if Lair Bhan was right,
then by saving Moira he'd be saving everyone else too. So
he'd try it. Only . . . it sure was a lot to expect from one
underweight twelve-year-old kid!

He drew a shuddering breath. "I'll go," he told the
Druid. "I've got to try to help Moira. She tried to help me."
He looked imploringly at the man. "But I sure don't know
what I can do when I get there, Lair Bhan. I still don't
think I really have any kind of power."

70

The Druid smiled and clapped him on the shoulder. "Good for you, lad! It took courage to agree to do this, great courage! But I felt that the courage was there, just as I feel that the power is there. Don't worry."

He bent down and reached behind the log to pick up two objects—a curved silver horn suspended from a leather thong and a slim wooden staff as long as his body, wound around and around with carvings of leaves. "We must leave right now," he said. "The Danaan army is probably even now entering the Shadow, far to the west of here. They will camp for the night within the Shadow, and in the morning they will march to the Plain of Muytoureagh, which they should reach by midday. It is there that the Fomoiri host will be awaiting them for battle. You and I should reach the Shadow by nightfall, and although the Fomoiri will un-doubtedly do things to try to stop us, we too should be able to reach Muytoureagh by midday tomorrow, to play what part we can in the battle."

Rick frowned. "Wow, Lair Bhan, that sounds like a pretty long walk. Do you really think we can get there in time?"

The Druid grinned. "We shall not have to walk." He lifted the silver horn to his lips and blew a single, long, clear note that sang through the forest.

"What was that for?" wondered the boy.

"I have called the one who will take us swiftly on our journey," answered the Druid. He slung the horn over one shoulder, then picked up the bag of food and slung it over the other. "Will you carry our water bag, Rick?"

"Sure." Rick shoved the wooden stopper into the neck of the leathern bag and slipped the strap over his head, adjusting it comfortably on his shoulder. Then he froze, staring in

71

awe at the creature that suddenly came trotting into the glade.

At first he thought it was a magnificent white horse, then he realized it was actually a unicorn! Its body was the color of pure milk or new-fallen snow; its mane and tail were the soft, misty gray of a summer rain cloud; its cloven hoofs were silver, and a two-foot-long pearly horn spiraled up out of its forehead. It pranced gracefully to the Druid and nuzzled his neck. Smiling, he stroked its nose.

"This is Roydeg, most beautiful of beasts and swiftest of runners. It is he that I signaled to with the horn. He will bear us into the Shadow and beyond, and share with us whatever is to come." The Druid's face grew serious. "You see, he too has courage, and is willing to lay down his life to help keep the Middle Kingdom free."

Enthralled, Rick eagerly moved toward the beautiful animal. Turning to face him, it pawed at the ground with its front hoof, bobbed its head, and whickered. Thinking this might be a warning, Rick stopped in his tracks.

"Don't be afraid," said Lair Bhan. "He is saluting you, as a fellow warrior."

"Will he let me pet him?" asked the boy hopefully. At Lair Bhan's nod, Rick stepped forward again until he could run his hand down the unicorn's velvety neck. Its brown eyes looked into his, and there was distinct friendship in them, as well as intelligence. "Wow, he's really great," whispered Rick in awe.

"That he is, in many ways," acknowledged the Druid. "Let us now be on our way. Hold my staff a moment." He put both hands on the unicorn's back and lightly lifted himself onto it. "Hand up my staff, then I'll help you mount behind me. You must hold fast to my waist, for when Roydeg runs, he can outdistance the wind itself."

Rick quickly found that wasn't much of an exaggeration. As soon as the unicorn felt that they were both settled securely on its back it was off like a shot. Rick could not imagine how the animal was able to move so swiftly and surely among the close-growing trees, but it almost seemed to flow through them, so that the forest was literally a blur to the boy's eyes. Surely, there was something magical about it! Rick wanted to ask questions, but he actually felt that his voice would simply be left behind by Roydeg's speed. In silence he hung on, his arms wrapped about Lair Bhan's waist, his legs gripping Roydeg's sides. He noticed that the forest seemed to be growing darker.

In what was surely less than an hour, they emerged from the forest onto the great meadow, and Rick realized that the day was nearly over, for dusk lay upon the sea of tall grass. Even so, the boy could see the great wall of darkness in the distance up ahead, and he knew without being told that this was the Shadow of Fomor. A thrill of excitement and apprehension coursed through his body.

Roydeg moved over the meadow in a smooth, steady gallop that ate up the distance as fast, it seemed to Rick, as a high-powered automobile. The eagle, Neamh Suil, had left Lair Bhan's shoulder and was flying a short distance above, at a pace that matched that of the unicorn. The dark wall of the Shadow drew steadily closer.

When they were nearly upon it, Lair Bhan leaned forward and said something to the unicorn, which slowed down and came to a halt. The eagle continued on into the Shadow and vanished from sight.

"Neamh Suil will scout ahead for us and make sure no sudden ambush awaits us as we enter the Shadow," Lair Bhan said over his shoulder to Rick. He turned around to look at the boy. "You may be sure that the Fomoiri are aware of our coming and will try to stop us, Rick. Most of their force is probably concentrated at Muytoureagh, awaiting the coming of the Danaan army, but they have many creatures at their beck and call that they could send against us. We will be in peril from the moment we enter the Shadow, but we will have the eyes of Neamh Suil, the speed of Roydeg, and my *draoidheacht*—my magic—to protect us."

They waited for a time, then the eagle reappeared, flying low out of the Shadow. It alighted on the Druid's shoulder and put its beak close to his ear. Rick could hear no sound, but after a moment Lair Bhan said, "Neamh Suil reports there is no sign of any living thing for some distance. Let us enter, then."

At his words, the unicorn broke into a trot. Within seconds they passed from twilight into full night. Yet the darkness within the Shadow was not as black as Rick had expected it to be. There was no moonlight in the murky sky, only a kind of grayish luminescence to the darkness, and the boy found, after a time, that he could make out the appearance of the ground over which they were passing. When they came abreast of a solitary, bare tree standing a short distance away on the plain, Rick could see it as a black silhouette against the just slightly lighter sky.

"Let us make camp here," said Lair Bhan softly, and the unicorn halted. "It is as good a place as any, and somehow that tree provides a slight touch of cheer in all this bleakness. We will not lose any time by camping for the night, for the Danaan army is probably no farther into the Shadow than we are, and it is encamped, too."

He slid down from the unicorn's back, followed by Rick. Bending down, the Druid began to walk about, pulling up a handful of dead grass here, a small twig there. Realizing what he was doing, Rick began to help, and shortly they had piled together enough twigs and brush for a small fire. To Rick's amazement and delight, Lair Bhan set this ablaze simply by pointing the end of his staff at it. Suddenly realizing how chilled he was, the boy squatted down to warm his hands before the blaze.

Struck by a thought, he looked up at the black shape of the Druid, standing nearby. "Won't it be dangerous to have a fire, though?" he asked. "You could probably see it miles away."

"It doesn't matter," said Lair Bhan. "The Fomoiri know we are here. The fire will help keep us warm and will help keep our spirits up. And I can do something to prevent anything from coming upon us unaware during the night."

Moving a short distance out from the fire, he began to pace slowly around it in a circle, chanting softly. When he had gone full circle, he returned and seated himself cross-legged beside the tiny, flickering blaze. "I have set a warding spell around us. We can go in and out of the circle, but nothing else can, without a powerful counter-spell that no one but a Fomoiri high wizard would know. Do not leave the area of the fire and you will be in no danger."

Spreading open the food bag, he handed Rick a loaf, a chunk of cheese, and a few strips of meat. He handed a single strip up to Neamh Suil, perched on his shoulder, and then began to munch on a loaf of bread himself.

"There's nothing for Roydeg," observed Rick, with some

concern. "He can't eat this dead, dry grass that's on the ground."

The unicorn gave a series of faint whickers and snorts. "He says that he filled himself up with food and water in the forest, before he joined us," Lair Bhan translated, "but he thanks you for your consideration." For the first time Rick realized, with astonishment, that the unicorn could not only understand human speech but could even converse, in his own way.

When they had finished eating, and shared swigs of water from the water bag, Lair Bhan lay down close to the fire. "Let us get all the sleep we can," he suggested. "Our bodies need to be rested and replenished for whatever we face tomorrow, and that is the purpose of sleep."

Following suit, Rick lay down, hugging himself for warmth, and closed his eyes. But he soon found that sleep was not going to come easily. He was too filled with apprehension, not only for himself and what might happen to him on the morrow, but also for Moira, and for Nion and Faol, too, for they were his friends. What had the Fomoiri done to them by now? He hoped they were all right, even though they were captives.

He was also concerned about his parents. He had been here in the Middle Kingdom for about two and a half days now, and Mom and Dad were probably crazy with worry. So were Moira's folks, without a doubt. The worst of it is, thought the boy, that if this "power" Lair Bhan thinks I have *doesn't* show up and beat the Fomoiri, my folks and Moira's folks will never see us again. We'll either be dead or enslaved here for the rest of our lives!

Sighing worriedly, he opened his eyes and looked at his companions. Lair Bhan appeared to be asleep. Neamh Suil

76

was perched on the man's hip, head bent down and tucked beneath a wing. Roydeg stood motionless, head down and eyes closed. Rick had a faint memory of having read, somewhere, that that was how horses slept. It looked as if no one but Rick was too keyed up and worried to sleep.

He noticed that the tiny fire had nearly burned itself out. As long as I'm awake maybe I could put more wood or brush on it, thought Rick. He glanced at the lone tree nearby, wondering if there might not be some twigs or broken branches lying beneath it. Don't leave the area of the fire, Lair Bhan had said, and the tree *was* outside the protective circle the Druid had set up, but no more than a dozen or so steps. Rick peered carefully about on all sides, but could detect no furtive movement or unexplainable shape anywhere on the flat surroundings. All seemed safe enough.

Quietly, he rolled to his feet and tiptoed toward the tree. Yes, he could see that there appeared to be quite a litter of branches beneath it. They formed a sizeable mound.

Reaching the pile, he stooped over and picked up a large branch from the top. It felt odd. It didn't have the rough texture of bark—it was smooth, as if all the bark had been peeled off it. Running his hand along its length he found that it had a bumpy knob at each end. It didn't *feel* like a branch, he decided. He peered at it, straining his eyes in the darkness. Suddenly, with a shock, he realized what it was. It was a long bone, like the arm or leg bone of a human skeleton.

Abruptly, a black mass at the foot of the tree, which he had taken for part of the tree trunk, seemed to uncoil itself and lean toward him. It seized his wrist in a grip that felt like a steel trap!

❧12❧

RICK YELPED IN FRIGHT, and an instant later the unicorn gave a screaming whicker. Suddenly, a burst of light from behind reached past him and bathed the tree in its glow. At the sight of the thing holding him in its grip, the boy gasped in horror.

It was tall, not as tall as a Brollachan, but taller than most humans, and although its body was swathed in some kind of tattered black garment, the boy could see that it was as gaunt as a Bodach. The hand that gripped his wrist extended from a bare arm that was nothing more than bone covered with skin. Its face, framed in a spreading tangle of spiky, grayish hair, looked vaguely human, with a long, hooked nose and an equally long, pointed chin. But the tips of two sharp fangs protruded down from its thin upper lip, and it appeared to have only one eye, a glowing bulbous disk to the left of its nose. Its skin was a pallid bluish color. It was seated with its legs drawn up, knees poking up on each side of its head, on a large pile of human bones.

"Release him, Annis Dubh!" Rick heard Lair Bhan shout.

"Too late, Druid," rasped the creature, in a voice that sounded like the creaky mumblings of some incredibly old woman. "I have him, and he is mine." The tiny mouth widened in a grin that fully displayed the sharp fangs. "I shall take him to my bower and skin him with these." It held up its free hand, and Rick saw that the fingers were tipped with black talons, like thin, sharp razors. "I will hang his skin up on the wall, with all the thousands of others, and I will feast on his sweet, young flesh. There is nothing more to be said."

"Yes there is, *cailleac*," said Lair Bhan, now standing beside Rick. "I challenge you to the Contest, Annis. If I win, you give up the lad. If I lose, you have us both."

The creature threw back its head and cackled with derisive laughter. "Begin then, *amadan*," it invited.

"What grows with its roots upward in winter, and cannot grow at all in summer?" said Lair Bhan.

Rick stared at him. What was happening here? It sounded as if Lair Bhan was asking the creature a *riddle*! "What are you doing?" he asked in a quavering voice, wincing from the pain of the hard, icy grip on his wrist.

"It is the ancient Riddling Contest," said Lair Bhan, softly. "No creature, mortal or magical, can refuse it if challenged, and both contestants *must* abide by the outcome. If I can ask her a riddle she cannot answer, she will release you."

Yeah, thought Rick, but if she asks *you* a riddle *you* can't answer, we're both dead! "I sure hope you know lots of riddles," he whispered.

"I do. I am accounted a Riddle Master, as are most Druids. But—she may well know more! She is thousands and thousands of years old, Rick. She is the last daughter of creatures that lived on earth long before humans ever appeared. Her wisdom is vast."

Annis had already solved Lair Bhan's riddle. "An icicle," she said, then intoned a riddle of her own.

"There may be a houseful or a holeful
but you cannot keep a bowlful."

"Smoke," said the Druid, with a quickness that gave Rick hope, and took his turn.

"Runs all day, but never walks.
Murmurs often, but never talks.
It has a bed, but never sleeps.
It has a mouth, but never eats."

Annis pondered for only a moment or two. "A river," she said, and immediately fired back her next challenge.

"A king gave to a queen
a container without lid or bottom
to keep flesh and blood in.
What was it?"

Lair Bhan stroked his chin thoughtfully and was silent. As the silence lengthened, Rick began to worry. But then, the Druid gave the answer.

"A ring for her finger."

On and on the contest went, back and forth, Annis riddling and Lair Bhan answering, the Druid riddling and Annis replying, until Rick felt sure hours had passed. But as time went on, the boy began to grow worried again. Annis answered most of Lair Bhan's riddles right away, but Rick noticed that the Druid was taking more and more time to answer hers. And Lair Bhan was clearly concerned. In the light that glowed from the tip of the Druid's staff, Rick could see that the man's face was covered with a film of perspiration, despite the chill air of the Shadow, and that his expression was grim. It's just as he said, thought Rick— she's lived so long that she probably knows a lot more riddles

80

than he does, and now she's starting to ask some he doesn't know, and he has to figure them out. That's hard—and dangerous! One bad guess and we're dead!

But even though she's lived thousands of years, thought the boy, she's been here in the Middle Kingdom most of the time, cut off from the outside world. There must be lots of new riddles she's never heard, and that Lair Bhan has never heard either, for that matter. All these riddles that he and she are asking each other are really all just *disguises* for things, like "a red deer on a hill" standing for the sunrise, and "a white barn with no door" standing for an egg. There's not really any trick or catch to any of them. I wonder if—

And then he had it. The Druid had just given an answer, and was mopping his brow before taking his turn to ask a riddle. "Lair Bhan," said Rick, "can I ask her the next one?"

The man looked at him for a moment, then nodded. "Go ahead. At least it will give me time to think."

Rick looked into the creature's glowing eyes. "Annis," he said boldly, "how many times can you subtract the number two from the number fifty?"

Lair Bhan looked disappointed and Annis snickered. "You seek to tease me with schoolboy sums, child?" she said with a confidence in her voice that made Rick's heart sink. But then he saw that her lips were moving and she was twiddling the fingers of her free hand, as if she were counting, and his hope grew.

"Twenty-five times," she said after a few moments, smirking at him.

"NO!" yelled Rick triumphantly. "The answer is *once*! Because once you take the number two from fifty, *it isn't fifty anymore*, it's forty-eight!"

Annis stared at him. Then she opened her mouth and gave vent to a long, drawn-out howl of fury that slowly began to die away as if she were falling swiftly into a deep pit. And as the howl faded, Annis seemed to dwindle and fade until, abruptly, she was gone, her pile of bones was gone, her grip on Rick's wrist was gone.

"Praise to Danu," said Lair Bhan, looking joyfully at the boy. "Rick, you have just saved yourself and me. I was running out of both riddles and answers! I never heard anything such as you asked her; where did you come by it?"

Rick let his breath whoosh out of his lips, and sank shakily to a sitting position. "A year ago I went to a summer camp," he said, looking up at the man and massaging the wrist that had been in Annis's grip. "That's a place where lots of boys go to spend the summer. One of the guys had a book of puzzles, and every night before bed he'd read a few and we'd try to figure them out. I remembered that one, and I thought that maybe old Annis wouldn't be sharp enough to spot the trick in it. And thank goodness, she wasn't!"

He was elated that he had been able to conquer the creature, and also felt quite proud of himself. But then, as the realization began sinking in of how close to death he had been and what Annis would have done to him had she won the contest, he shivered violently in horror, and grew sober. He was ashamed to think that both he and Lair Bhan had been at risk of death simply because he hadn't obeyed the Druid's urging to stay inside the protective magical circle.

"This was all my fault," he said regretfully. "I'm sorry, Lair Bhan. You *told* me to stay by the fire and I didn't. I wanted to get more wood for it, and I thought I could just quickly go to the tree and pick some up. I could have sworn she wasn't there when I started toward it."

"I am sure that she wasn't," the Druid told him. "Annis has the power to suddenly appear where she knows she can seize her prey, and the Fomoiri instructed her to make you her victim. When you left the circle, she sensed it instantly, and came to the tree." He patted the boy's shoulder. "Do not blame yourself too much, Rick. It is simply that such things no longer happen in your world, and you do not know about them. Long years ago, in the places you now call Ireland, Scotland, and northern England, all children knew of Annis, and knew they must be careful to stay out of her grasp. Such things are now mostly forgotten or spoken of only in jest in your world, but *here* you must take care constantly, Rick, for here, the evil things that are naught but legends in your world are real, and they are the servants of Fomor." He hesitated a moment, then continued. "I feel I must tell you, lad, that the danger to you has grown great. It is clear that now that the Fomoiri are sure it is only you they must fear, they have decided to seek your death!"

The unicorn snorted softly, and Lair Bhan glanced toward him and nodded. "Roydeg thinks we should return within the circle, and he is right. The Fomoiri know by now that Annis failed in her purpose, and you may be sure they will try to strike again, in some other way."

There were, as Rick had suspected, many broken branches and twigs scattered around the tree, and Lair Bhan scooped up a bundle of them. With Neamh Suil on his shoulder, Rick at his side, and Roydeg pacing behind, he strode back to the pile of ashes that marked the site of the fire and quickly started a new blaze with the wood he had collected. He then spoke a word, and the glow of light that spread out from the tip of his staff vanished. Once again, he and Rick lay down beside the fire, the eagle tucked its head

83

under its wing, and the unicorn planted his feet, lowered his head, and closed his eyes.

Despite the terror he had been through, Rick now felt very sleepy, and he wondered if perhaps Lair Bhan had put some sort of spell on him to help him sleep. But his thoughts before he drifted into slumber were of the Druid's last words—"The Fomoiri know by now that Annis failed in her purpose, and you may be sure they will try to strike again, in some other way." What way? wondered the boy. His sleep, when it came, was not restful, and he dreamed of dark, furtive shapes with glowing eyes and razor-sharp talons that lurked menacingly all around him.

❧13❧

MOIRA COULDN'T STOP SHIVERING, even though Faol was cuddling her against his side and had wrapped both arms around her for warmth. She, Nion, Faol, and the other Danaan warriors were being held in a cave of which the walls, floor, and ceiling were formed of grayish, rock-hard ice, and the air was so cold that as they breathed, little clouds of vapor emerged from their mouths and noses. Moira's clothing, suitable for an Irish summer, was no protection against such near-freezing cold.

But she wasn't shivering only from the cold, Moira admitted to herself. She was thoroughly terrified. When she had determined to set out on the search for Rick, she had not thought about what being captured by the Fomoiri would actually mean. She had figured they were probably like the terrorists she had heard of in her own world, who took innocent people hostage or killed them with bombs, but she had felt she could stand up to such persons if need be. She hadn't understood how alien and horrible the Fomoiri actually were!

She had been examined by several of the creatures while her companions lay nearby, helpless under the paralyzing enchantment that had been cast over them. The Fomoiri had not caused Moira any pain, nor were they the least bit

85

rough with her, but their examination had been the most hideous experience of her life up to now. They had simply stared into her eyes and lightly fingered the sides of her head, but she had felt exactly as if she were buried in a sea of icy-cold worms that were crawling over and *through* her entire body by the millions! She had felt that she actually wanted to die and bring the horror to an end, but then thought that surely must be a sin, so she had closed her eyes and prayed for deliverance.

It had finally come. Suddenly the Fomoiri seemed to become totally uninterested in her, as if they had found her to be a thing of no value. They had turned away from her, and a group of Brollachans waiting nearby had come forward, picked up Moira and her companions, and carried them all through dark, winding tunnels to the icy cave, into which they had been tossed like so many sacks of potatoes into a grocery store bin. But at least the metal rings of enchantment had been removed from all the Danaan warriors and the Luchorpan, and now they were gradually regaining the use of their bodies and came to the assistance of the sobbing, shivering girl.

"Ah, Nion was right and I was wrong to let you come with us," said Faol in a voice steeped in bitterness. "I did not dream we could be captured so easily. No maiden should have torment such as this put upon her!"

But Moira shook her head. Throughout everything that had happened to her in the Shadow up to now she had continued to feel the same way—that, for some mysterious reason, she was *needed* there. "I still think that I have to be here," she said. "There's some reason for me to be here, although I don't know what it is."

"Well, at least we now know that it isn't to be of any use to

86

the Fomoiri, nor to be any danger to them," croaked Nion. He was sitting cross-legged, his arms wrapped around himself, hands gripping his shoulders and chin buried in the crook of one elbow. "It was plain to see that they found you weren't the one they were seeking after all. That's good news for the Danaan cause and good news for you, for I think that if they had feared you for any reason, you would now be dead!"

"Yes, it's Rick they wanted after all," said Moira. "But they haven't got him. I wonder where he is?"

"Wandering about, lost in the Coil Mor, I fear," said Nion.

Teine shook his head. "If he is in the Great Forest, Lair Bhan will have found him by now. The Druid knows of every leaf that falls in the Coil Mor."

"Then maybe he's safe at least," said Moira. "I'm glad of that." She hesitated a moment and then said in a small voice, "Is there any hope for *us* though, I wonder?"

An uncomfortable silence followed her question, and Faol hurried to fill it. "There is always hope while we yet live, *cailin*. Sooner or later the High King will move against the Fomoiri, and if Dagda grants victory to the Danaan army we shall be saved and freed."

"And if the Danaan are defeated," said Nion, "we shall be no worse off than anyone else in the Middle Kingdom." He grinned. "So you see, things can only get better."

No sooner were the words out of his mouth than he was proven wrong. There was a sound of shuffling footsteps in the tunnel that led to the cave, and half a dozen giant yellow Brollachans appeared, accompanied by a Fomor in black scale armor. The Brollachans bore odd-looking harnesses made of black leather, and despite fierce struggling, the

87

Danaan warriors were slipped into these, as were Moira and Nion. The Brollachans then hauled the captives out of the cave and began dragging them through the tunnel.

"What are they going to do? Where are they taking us?" cried Moira, but none of the others could tell her.

After a time they suddenly emerged into the twilight that filled the sky within the Shadow, and found themselves in a kind of broad courtyard of the eerie fortress to which they had been brought by the *púca*-riding Fomoiri who had captured them. A number of two-wheeled vehicles that looked to Moira like chariots were lined up in a row stretching across the courtyard, and to all but one of them a variety of dispirited-looking animals were harnessed—horses, deer, bears, and several creatures that Moira recognized with astonishment as unicorns. The ribs of all these animals stood out from starvation, their heads drooped, and their eyes were dull.

To the dismay of Moira and her companions, they were pulled straight toward the chariot that had no beasts harnessed to it, and they realized that *they* were to be its team of draft animals. Despite the frenzied struggles of the Danaan they were harnessed into place in two rows, on each side of a long pole that jutted from the front of the chariot, with Moira at the head of one row and Nion leading the other.

"I will die before I become your beast of burden!" howled the warrior known as Oisin, writhing in his bonds. The others shouted in agreement, and also began to struggle with their harnesses. But the armored Fomor glided toward Moira, and the warriors froze, fearful that he intended to harm her. He spoke, in a throaty, snarling voice that dripped with menace.

"I am Goll, Chieftain of Fomor. You will obey my will in

88

all things, or this one"—he touched a thin finger to Moira's head—"will suffer such pain that it will plead for a death that never comes."

The Danaan warriors looked at one another and their faces hardened. They ceased tearing at the leather straps that bound them, and stood in silence.

The Fomor stepped up into the chariot and took the reins that led to the harnessed people. "Forward," he barked.

Ahead of them, Brollachans were pushing open a wide gate in the black, ice-covered wall of the fortress. Leaning forward and digging their feet into the ground, the seven prisoners strained to start the chariot moving. With a dull rumbling of wheels it complied, and they headed toward the gate. The other chariots, each also occupied by an armored Fomor, swung into line behind the leader.

A vast army had gathered outside the fortress wall. Rank upon rank of mummylike Bodachs, armed with stone-tipped spears and leather shields, stood chattering with one another; hundreds of yellow Brollachans with wooden clubs and wooden-hafted stone axes squatted in stolid silence; scores of red-eyed *púcas* paced and prowled with red tongues lolling out of their mouths. A cluster of twenty-foot giants, clad in furs, wielded a variety of huge weapons. Their skin was gray and warty, and their faces were coarse and brutal. Moira and the Danaan spied groups of other monstrous creatures as they hauled the chariot of Goll out onto the great, bleak plain that stretched away from the black Fomoiri fortress.

"Straight ahead," ordered Goll. "Move faster."

A kind of shuffling trot was the best they could do, but it seemed to satisfy the Fomor. The other chariots moved out and arranged themselves alongside that of the leader, and with a great rumbling of many feet, the army of horrors came surging along behind. A dark gray mist hung low over it. The sky had turned pitch black, and bright bolts of lightning snaked and flared through it. The ground over which the Fomoiri chariots rolled turned white with chilling frost.

The march across the plain probably took no more than half an hour, but it was the most pain-filled ordeal of Moira's young life. Her feet and legs gradually became aching lumps, and the small of her back burned with pain because of her constant hunched-over position. She would have fallen many times but for the help of Nion, who had stretched out a hand to support her and help keep her moving. With her teeth clenched and her eyes closed, she concentrated on simply moving her feet, one after another, trying to ignore the pain because she knew that if she stopped or even lagged, the silver-eyed creature in the chariot might subject her to much stronger pain than this!

Still, her pain grew worse. When she felt she simply could not keep going, she heard Faol's voice from behind her. "The host of Danaan!" he exclaimed.

Moira opened her eyes. Ahead, perhaps less than a mile distant, was a throng of tiny figures, above which fluttered numerous banners. It's the Danaan army, she thought, and hope flared within her. They've come to fight the Fomoiri. We'll be saved!

The distance lessened until Moira could begin to make out individual figures in the front rank of the Danaan army, and soon she was able to see distinct faces and the emblems on shields. The two armies were no more than a hundred yards apart.

"Halt," croaked Goll.

Sobbing with relief, Moira dropped to a sitting position on the frozen ground, and turned her head to look behind her. Her heart sank as she saw how far across the plain the army of Fomor extended, and she realized that the Danaan were vastly outnumbered. She was struck by the terrifying thought that the Danaan might lose the battle that was obviously going to be fought, and that she might spend the rest of her life as she was now—a beast of burden for merciless masters. For the first time in her life she truly understood what it was like to be a slave or a hostage of terrorists.

Out of the black sky a cold, driving sleet came rushing, guided by a howling wind to slant almost horizontally into the face of the Danaan army. The air was turning bitterly chill. Lightning bolts were striking the plain, shattering into flaring fountains of sparks and leaving smoking black smudges. Moira realized that she was seeing the terrible power of the Fomoiri.

And at that moment, without any warning, the Fomoiri assumed their true shapes.

The girl shrieked in horror, and even the hardened warriors sprawled on the ground around her gasped. The man-like, black-clad Goll had vanished, and in his place in the chariot was a hideous man-tall, wormlike thing. A pair of thick, short tentacles protruded on one side of its cylindrical body, and a cluster of three projected out on the other side. High up on its tapering head bulged a single silver eye, beneath which was a lipless V-shaped mouth. The creature was a pallid, blotchy gray in color.

It spoke in a voice that boomed across the plain.

"Danaan! Your cause is hopeless. Cast down your weapons and desist from your magical spells. Submit, and we shall let you live. Resist, and we shall wipe you out, destroy your cities, and give your females and young ones to our servants, to be their slaves—and food!"

The warriors of the Danaan army stirred and scowled but made no reply to the Fomorian.

Goll spoke again. "You think there is hope for you. You think that the man-child we sought in the other world, and those who are aiding it, will come to put its power to the test against us. It will not! We sent one against it which failed, but now we have sent one against which it cannot prevail. It is doomed!"

He's talking about Rick, Moira realized with horror. Somewhere, Rick was in even worse danger than she was here. He might even be dead already!

She lowered her head, her eyes welling with tears. There was no hope—for him, for her, for anyone.

The Danaan had still made no reply to Goll's words. Clearly, they were prepared to fight to the death rather than surrender.

"Very well," snarled the monster in the chariot. With a sound like the rumble of distant thunder, the army of Fomor went rushing to the attack.

❧14❧

RICK LAY AWAKE on his back, staring up into the black sky, when what passed for dawn in the eternal twilight of the Shadow began to dispel some of the night's darkness.

His thoughts were seething. He knew that this might well be the last day of his life, but if he did manage to survive, it would probably be the most momentous day of his entire life, even if he lived another sixty or seventy years. The fate of two worlds was in his hands, according to Lair Bhan, and if this power that the Druid thought he possessed revealed itself as it was supposed to, then he, Rick McNeese, would be the one to save both worlds from the horror of the Fomoiri.

Actually, he was really much more concerned about saving Moira. If the Fomoiri would send a horrible creature such as Annis to murder him, what might they do to the helpless girl who was in their hands? If his "power" could save two worlds, that was great, but what he mainly wanted to do was rescue his cousin!

Only—he still didn't think he really had any kind of power. Certainly, no power had sprung forth to protect him from Annis; nothing but dumb luck in remembering a trick question had saved him from a horrible death at her hands.

Would dumb luck be enough to save Moira? It hardly seemed likely.

He clenched his teeth. Well, whatever happens will happen, he told himself. I just want to get it all over with! I'll wake up Lair Bhan and tell him I want to get going!

But as he sat up abruptly and looked toward the Druid, he saw that the man was awake and watching him. "You wish to hurry to the conclusion of our journey, whatever it may be, do you not?" asked Lair Bhan, revealing that he knew what was in Rick's mind. He rose lithely to his feet, holding stiff the arm upon which Neamh Suil was perched, so as not to dislodge the bird. "Let us be off, then."

They gulped down a hasty breakfast of what remained in the food bag and then, within minutes, they were racing over the bleak plain on the back of the galloping unicorn. Neamh Suil had launched himself into the air and was flying far ahead of them, lost to their sight in the dark sky, to scout the way for danger.

The morning lengthened and the blackness of the night gave way completely to the "day" of twilight. Roydeg's hoofs drummed tirelessly over the hard ground of the plain.

Then, suddenly, Neamh Suil was streaking toward them, uttering what sounded to Rick like frantic screams of warning!

"Danu!" exclaimed Lair Bhan, in either a prayer or a curse.

"What is it, what's the matter?" asked Rick, alarmed by the concern in the man's voice.

"We are about to be attacked," said the Druid. "Hang on tightly, we will have to depend upon Roydeg's speed and agility to save us."

Rick started to ask who was going to attack them, but

what came out of his mouth was a wordless shout of horror, as the attacker suddenly became visible, rushing toward them out of the dark sky. It was as big as the jet airplane that had taken Rick and his parents to Ireland, and it was moving at such tremendous speed that it quickly seemed to fill the entire sky. Breathtakingly beautiful yet also frighteningly horrible, it was covered with pebbly green scales that sparkled like emeralds, and its body bristled with sharp spines and spikes and daggerlike talons. Curved, pointed teeth that were as long as Rick's whole body protruded from its wide, lipless mouth, and its immense eyes were a murky amber-yellow. No creature such as this had ever existed in Rick's world, but there were enough stories and legends and artists' renditions of such a creature that Rick knew that he was staring at a live, monstrous flying dragon.

He expected Roydeg to turn and try to outrun the giant reptile, but to his surprise the unicorn kept galloping straight on toward the creature, not even increasing speed. The dragon stiffened its wings and glided, dropping lower until it was no more than fifteen or twenty feet above the ground and rapidly closing in upon them, first a hundred yards away . . . seventy yards away . . . fifty yards away. Its mouth yawned open.

Instantly, with the smoothness of flowing quicksilver, Roydeg changed direction and, in a burst of speed, galloped away at a sharp right angle. A split second later, with an ear-piercing hiss like the sound of a giant tea kettle, a flare of flame shot from the dragon's mouth and seared the earth in the exact spot the unicorn had just left. The speed of the dragon's glide carried it hurtling onward, and a bellow of rage at having missed its target came drifting back.

Roydeg changed direction again, now heading the way he

had been going originally. Craning his neck, Rick saw the dragon turn in a great curve, beating its wings to gain speed, and come streaking after them, growing larger with alarming swiftness. Its yellow eyes glared straight into his, and to his horror he found that he could not look away. Again the giant reptile opened its mouth to spurt forth flame, and its eyes seemed to promise Rick that within moments he would become a smoking, blackened husk.

But Roydeg, watching the dragon's approach over his shoulder, stopped with such suddenness that Rick slammed into Lair Bhan's back. At that very moment the dragon belched forth an orange burst of flame that struck the ground precisely where the unicorn would have been if it had kept on running. The reptile shot on past overhead, and the wind of its passage was like the push of a giant invisible hand, causing Roydeg to stagger to keep his footing.

But as the dragon passed overhead, Lair Bhan struck back. He raised his staff and a streak of white-hot energy snapped from the tip of it and sizzled into the underside of the huge reptile's body, leaving a large splotch of black among the sparkling emerald-green scales. The dragon howled in pain and fury, making the air quiver, and banked off to the left, beating its wings to gain altitude. Roydeg once again galloped straight ahead.

The dragon made another broad turn and came driving back at them from the side this time. Rick realized that Roydeg would have a harder time eluding an attack from this angle. The unicorn would not be able to turn aside in either direction, for the dragon's flame would catch it coming or going. The tactic of stopping suddenly might not work either, the boy saw with concern.

But as the dragon closed in on them it suffered a sudden

distraction. Neamh Suil came swooping out of the sky with the speed of a shooting star. The eagle was dwarfed by its foe, like an ant against an elephant, but its attack was devastating nevertheless, for with beak and talons it slashed and tore at one of the dragon's great golden eyes. The dragon shrieked and swerved and emitted a blast of flame that flared harmlessly through the air. For a moment, the whole underside of its body was a huge target silhouetted against the sky, and Lair Bhan quickly launched another bolt from his staff. This time the burst of energy struck an outspread wing, burning a great ragged hole in it. The dragon screamed again and turned away. To Rick, its flight seemed slower and somewhat erratic.

"It's hurt!" he exulted.

"Yes, it is in pain, crippled, and, I suspect, running out of flame, for it cannot belch forth fire too often without using up its body's resources for a time," said Lair Bhan. "We have a good chance!"

The dragon swung around and came at them again, this time from an angle to the side and rear. Roydeg began to run in zigzag fashion, making sudden changes in direction, galloping at right angles and in curves, and altering his speed. The dragon, forced to constantly change its course, was having a hard time. Finally, it bellowed in anger, and breathed out a brief blast of fire that fell far short of the target.

"Indeed, it has used up most of its fire," said Lair Bhan with satisfaction. "Now it will have to resort to teeth and claws, which means it will have to get close enough to seize us, and that will give me the best chance we shall have to destroy it!" He bared his teeth in a grim smile, and Rick suddenly noticed how drawn and haggard he looked. "I, too, am nearly out of fire, for the spell that draws lightning out of a quiet sky and sends it forth from my staff also draws upon the life and strength of the one who uses it. I have power for only one more blast, but with the luck of Dagda, that will be enough!"

The dragon was climbing, flapping its wings to gain height, and it was soon lost to sight high in the dark sky. Roydeg began running smoothly in a straight path, to give Lair Bhan as steady a perch as possible. Clutching his staff, the Druid peered upward, waiting.

"There it is!" yelled Rick.

The dragon was stooping upon them, as a bird of prey stoops upon the unsuspecting creature far beneath it, with wings folded tightly against its body, dropping like a stone, its front legs stiffly extended and taloned claws spread wide. Staring up at it, Rick saw its eyes become yellow pinheads, then the size of peas, then button-sized, then baseball-sized. Again, he found himself unable to look away from them, and they seemed to speak to him. *You can do nothing*, they said. *You are helpless. You cannot move. Accept your fate. Accept your swift death!*

But Lair Bhan knew the enchantment of a dragon's eyes, and knew better than to gaze directly into them. He focused his own eyes slightly to one side, seeing the growing shape of the dragon's body only as a dark-green blur in the corner of his vision. He knew that before it struck it would unfurl its wings to brake its fall at the last moment, and an instant later its talons would seize its prey. But at the moment it spread its wings he would have a split second in which to loose the blast of power from his staff. He could not dare look directly at the creature until that split second, and if he misjudged the moment or missed his aim, then he and Rick and Roydeg would be torn to bits in an instant.

His mouth frozen open in a silent yell of terror and his eyes wide and unblinking, Rick saw the dragon's hideous head grow and grow, like a mask that was moving toward him until it filled his entire field of vision. Its jaws were open and its huge teeth bared, and its murky yellow eyes burned straight into his, promising death. He could not move, he could only wait, like a mouse frozen by the hypnotic gaze of a snake slithering toward it. He became aware that the dragon had suddenly spread its wings.

And then, its head vanished in an explosion of white fire. Rick's body jerked as the spell of enchantment was abruptly broken, and he turned his head to see the dragon's body slam into the ground, no more than a dozen yards behind the unicorn's flying hoofs. The great green form seemed to shatter and lose its shape, like a balloon pricked by a pin. It lay in a vast heap on the gray plain, and in the twilight of the Shadow, it looked like a sprawling pile of green pebbles, out of which the white shaft of a shattered bone protruded here and there, and from which a dark, smoking liquid oozed out of cracks and rents.

Roydeg cantered to a stop some twenty yards farther and solemnly turned his head to survey the dead enemy. Neamh Suil came gliding out of the sky and settled upon Lair Bhan's shoulder.

"That was a very near thing," said the Druid softly. He took a deep breath and shook himself. "Well, we have met the strongest challenge the Fomoiri could throw against us and we have beaten it! Few can say that they have bested a dragon!"

"I was no help," Rick said bitterly. "That power I'm supposed to have didn't show up to help this time, either. I didn't do anything."

Lair Bhan put a hand on the boy's shoulder. "Rick, *each* of us has played a part in winning this far. It was you who bested Annis when *I* was failing, and Neamh Suil and Roydeg could not have helped there at all. It took the speed and valor of Roydeg, the courage of Neamh Suil, and my skill with magic combined, to defeat the dragon. One of us, and probably even two of us, could not have done it alone. I thank the powers that sent us all on this journey together, for we could never have come this far without the help that each has given to the others.

"And now our journey is nearly over. Look there." He pointed northward. Looking in that direction, Rick saw that the distant sky was midnight black and laced with flickers of lightning. "That is the sky over Muytoureagh," said Lair Bhan, "and it shows that battle is even now being waged there. We shall arrive in less time than it takes to chop down a young tree. All that we have been through was but a prelude. Now comes the final encounter!"

❧15❧

ALTHOUGH THE SKY OVER THE PLAIN OF MUYTOUREAGH was as black as the middle of the night, the plain was illuminated by a weird, flickering luminescence produced by the scores of flaring lightning bolts snaking through the sky every second. It's like standing under a flashing electric sign, thought Rick.

Roydeg's hoofs drummed on the ground as he carried the man and boy toward the heart of the plain, but even above that steady sound could be heard a distant whispering roar that rose and fell. Rick knew without being told that this was the sound of battle. Ahead of them, the army of the Danaan was fighting the Fomor host. Men, Bodachs, and other creatures were shouting, screaming, and snarling; swords were clashing; clubs were slamming against shields; feet were shuffling and stamping; and the din from all of this reached Rick and Lair Bhan like the sound of distant surf surging against a rocky shore.

Although the moment for the confrontation with the Fomoiri was nearly at hand, Rick did not feel any differently from the way he had felt all through the last few days. There was no sign of any strange power beginning to surge within him. He was still, as he had insisted all along, just an ordinary twelve-year-old boy. However, much to his surprise, he wasn't afraid. He figured that maybe after being snatched out of his own world, held prisoner by two such monsters as the Bodach and Brollachan, facing starvation in a vast forest, and being threatened with death by the talons of the hag Annis and the fiery breath of a gigantic dragon, there wasn't much fear left in him. He still simply wanted to just get everything over with, once and for all. If the power that Lair Bhan thought he had would manifest itself somehow, and enable him to save Moira, that would be wonderful. But if, as he suspected, no such power existed, he would either get himself killed or enslaved by the Fomoiri, and at least all the uncertainty would finally end.

The din of battle was growing louder. Peering around Lair Bhan's back, Rick found that Roydeg was now close enough to the combat so that the armies were visible. He could not tell which side was which yet, could not even make out any individual figures—only a vast, seething mass that formed a great multicolored splotch on the frost-white plain. But as the unicorn continued to close the distance, his riders were able to discern more details. Lair Bhan's face grew grim, and Rick's eyes widened with dismay.

Surrounded, the Danaan army was fighting for its life. The pale-haired warriors had formed in a compact ring some three men deep, and the ground all around the ring was thick with the fallen bodies of both Danaan warriors and their foes. The army of Fomor had completely encircled the Danaan in a vast, milling mob, and from time to time portions of this mass would surge in against the ring of Danaan warriors to engage in hand-to-hand combat, then would sullenly fall back. Each time, the Danaan ring shrank.

Roydeg came to a stop no more than a hundred yards from the area of combat. The creatures of the Fomor army were so intent on pressing their attack against the Danaan that none of them noticed the unicorn and its two riders. Roydeg glanced over his shoulder at Lair Bhan as if asking the Druid what to do next. He pawed at the ground with his front hoofs and tossed his head repeatedly. Clearly, he would have liked nothing better than to lower his horn and go charging into the rear of the circle of Fomoiri creatures. Rick understood how he felt but also realized how useless that would be. The unicorn might stab a few foes with his horn, dispatch a few more with kicks of his sharp hoofs, but then he would be quickly hacked and stabbed to death by others. Lair Bhan might be able to summon enough power to blast some of the monsters with lightning from his staff, but he, too, would soon be overwhelmed by the sheer numbers of the creatures. As for me, Rick thought in anger and frustration, there's nothing *I* could do at all.

"It's no use, Lair Bhan," he said in a low voice. "Nothing's happening to me. I have no power. I can't help any."

The Druid looked at him but said nothing.

Dully, Rick studied the scene of battle. He noticed, now, that there were a number of chariots interspersed within the circle of the Fomor horde, and grimaced with disgust at the sight of the tentacled wormlike creatures that rode in them. He saw that the worm-things were giving orders to the Bodachs and Brollachans and other creatures, and he suddenly realized that the chariot riders were the Fomoiri in their true form. He shuddered. These were the things that wanted him in their power, and already had Moira!

Was she still alive? Was she being kept prisoner somewhere, or was she perhaps here, in one of the chariots? He peered hopefully into the milling array, picking out the chariots, praying that he'd see a red-haired girl in one.

Suddenly, he *did* see her, no more than some fifty yards away! But she was not in one of the chariots, she was crouched listlessly on the ground, fastened to a harness that led to one of the chariots, along with Nion, Faol, and a handful of Danaan warriors. With rising anger, Rick realized that she and the others were being made to pull the vehicle, like horses pulling a wagon. The Fomoiri had made his cousin a slave, a beast of burden!

"There she is!" he yelled. "I've got to help her!"

He slid down off Roydeg's back and started to run toward the throng of grotesque creatures. He heard Lair Bhan call his name, but he paid no attention. A terrible rage was burning within him. He wanted only to get to the Fomor that had harnessed Moira to its chariot, and attack it. He wanted to kill it!

But I have no weapon, he thought. I need something to stab or hit with. Then he remembered his so-called lucky piece, the heavy metal lump he carried in his pocket. At least it would lend weight to his fist if he struck at someone, or make a good missile for throwing. He tugged it out of his pocket and clutched it tightly in his fist.

He reached the edge of the Fomor army and found himself among a crowd of Bodachs that were excitedly hopping up and down and banging their spear shafts against their leather shields, making a booming noise. Their backs were to him, and he rushed through them, pummeling and thrusting aside any who got in his way. In a tiny corner of his mind he knew that they could stab him in the back with their spears, but in his rage to get to the Fomor who was mistreating Moira, such things as Bodach spears seemed unimportant. He was so angry that his body seemed to be burning. There was a shrill howling in his ears, and he

104

actually felt invincible. If the Bodachs knew what was good for them they would simply clear out of his way and cause no trouble!

To the surprise of that tiny corner of reason in his mind, the Bodachs *were* getting out of his way. Those ahead of him were turning around, their faces twisting with shock as they saw him rushing toward them, and their jaws opening to scream in terror. Making no attempt to stop him, they were actually scrambling to get out of his path. Absently, he noted that a glow of light was washing over all the Bodachs nearest him, as if torchlight or firelight touched them as he approached, and he suddenly realized, with no great surprise, that his entire body was glowing with a red-orange brilliance, like a metal bar slowly heating up in a fire. He knew that he was giving off both intense light and heat, although he felt nothing.

Now he was through the Bodachs and rushing into a cluster of wolflike, horse-sized *púcas*. Any one of them could have snatched him up with its great jaws and chewed him to pieces in an instant, but they merely stared at him with terror in their red eyes and quickly slunk out of his path, tails between their legs, as if they were no more than big dogs that had been scolded by a feared master.

He sped through crowds of other creatures that also quickly made way for him. Just once a giant Brollachan did try to seize him, but as its hand touched him, the entire creature burst into flame. He left it behind, a blackened, formless lump lying on the ground.

Abruptly, there was nothing between him and the chariot to which Moira and his friends were harnessed. The pallid gray, wormlike thing in the chariot was staring at him with its silvery eye. It lifted the reins and jerked at them savagely.

It's trying to get away, thought Rick. It's going to make Moira and the others drag it to safety!

He was so enraged that he was lighting up the air around him with a yellow-white glow as bright as noonday sunshine. Only the destruction of the thing in the chariot would cool down his fury. He knew what he had to do. Planting his feet widespread, he drew back his arm and with every bit of strength he could muster, hurled the metal lump in his hand at the Fomor.

As the chunk of metal left his hand it became a slim shaft of dazzling brilliance that sped through the air with a sizzling shriek. Unerringly toward the Fomor it flew, and struck the creature squarely on its body between the two clusters of tentacles. There was a tremendous burst of incandescence, as if, for just an instant, the sun had touched the earth. Then, where the Fomor had been, was nothing.

Slowly, Rick came back to himself. He was no longer glowing, and he felt quite cool and normal. A tremendous wailing sound echoed in his ears, and glancing about he saw that the Fomoiri and their creatures were fleeing in all directions, howling in anguish and fear. But from one direction there came loud and jubilant cheering. Rick turned around to look that way and beheld the Danaan army, the eyes of every warrior fixed upon him, waving their swords and shields in salute.

He suddenly became aware of something else, something he had not seen since he and Lair Bhan, Roydeg, and Neamh Suil had left the sunlit portion of the Middle Kingdom. He was casting a shadow. He looked upward. The sky overhead was bright blue and in the center of it triumphantly blazed the sun.

The Shadow of Fomor was gone.

❧16❧

I DID HAVE POWER AFTER ALL, Rick told himself in amazement. The Fomoiri were right to be afraid of me. I've beaten them! But—how did I do it?

Through the confusion of his thoughts and the din all around him, he suddenly heard a familiar voice calling his name, and looked about to see Moira, freed from the harness, dashing toward him. She flung herself upon him and enveloped him in a powerful hug. "I thought you were dead!" she exclaimed. "And then suddenly you came running through all those monsters, *glowing* as if there were a fire burning inside you! Then you threw that bolt of lightning at Goll and killed him! You've saved us all! But how did you do it? Where did you get such magic?"

Rick shook his head. "I'm darned if I know. I was just trying to figure it out myself." He regarded her thoughtfully. "It was as if something came over me when I saw what the Fomoiri had done to you. I was so mad, and I hated them so much, that it was like I was on fire and nothing could stop me. It was my lucky piece that I threw, but it changed from a piece of metal into a kind of fiery spear, or beam, like a laser. But *I* didn't make it happen. I don't know how it happened."

There was no chance for further conversation between

107

them, because they were suddenly surrounded by a mob of joyful Danaan warriors who all wanted to shake Rick's hand or clap him on the back. To his embarrassment, many of them knelt to him as if he were a great lord. Faol appeared, grinning, to give him a big bear hug, and a beaming Nion showed up to shake his hand. Then the warriors drew back respectfully as Lair Bhan made his way through the crowd, accompanied by another, older, orange-robed Druid.

"Rick!" Lair Bhan exclaimed, grinning and clapping the boy on the shoulder. "You did it! Thanks be to Danu I was right and there *was* a power within you. I could feel it growing as you ran toward the battle, then suddenly it *exploded* out of you!"

"Yes," said Rick, remembering. "It seemed to suddenly take over when I pulled my lucky piece out of my pocket."

"Lucky piece?" said Lair Bhan. "What is it?"

"It's just an old, round piece of metal I found in my basement one day in a box full of old stuff that Mom said had been in the family for generations," explained the boy. "It's sort of reddish-colored, like copper, and there's a design cut into it that looks like a sun with a face on it. That's what I threw at the Fomoiri."

The older Druid accompanying Lair Bhan stared at Rick with sudden comprehension. "The Tahthlum!" he exclaimed.

Lair Bhan, too, was looking at Rick with the expression of one for whom a great puzzle has suddenly been solved. "Of course! That explains everything."

"Do you mean the power was in my lucky piece?" asked Rick.

"Exactly," said Lair Bhan. "Do you know the story of the first battle of the Danaan against the Fomoiri, which took place thousands of years ago? The battle was won when Lugh the Fiery hurled the Tahthlum, the magical sun stone in which his power resided, at the Fomor king and destroyed him with a blast of light. That is exactly what happened today. Your 'lucky piece' could only have been the Tahthlum, and when you pitted yourself against the Powers of Darkness it filled you with the Power of Light, as it did to Lugh, long ago."

"But how come I had it?" wondered Rick. "How come my family had a magical thing like that?"

"The Tahthlum was never found after that first battle," said the older Druid. "It was always presumed that it destroyed itself when it destroyed the Fomor king, Balor of the Killing Eye. But it must be that it was actually lying on the battlefield, unseen by those who searched for it. And at some time in the thousands of years since the battle, someone found it and kept it." He smiled at the boy. "I understand that you come from that new land, far over the sea, but nevertheless the blood of Eriu is in you, for your ancestors were of the people of Eriu. There seems no doubt that it was one of them who found the Tahthlum and handed it down to his or her descendants as a keepsake, not knowing what it was, until it came into your hands to save us all."

Lair Bhan nodded. "I am sure that Caithbad is right," he said, indicating the older Druid. "And when you came to present-day Eriu—that is, Ireland—the Fomoiri sensed the presence of the Tahthlum and knew that it could destroy all their plans. They sought for it until they finally determined that either you or Moira had it, but they did not know which until they captured her and found that she neither had it nor knew of its existence. Then they tried to

eliminate you before you could use it against them, but"—
he grinned—"as we know, they were not successful."

"Fantastic!" said Rick, marveling at all this. "What a
coincidence that I just happened to find the Tahthlum after
all those years and that I came to Ireland with it just when
it was needed most."

Lair Bhan's face grew serious. "I doubt that it was merely
coincidence, Rick. The Powers of Light and Darkness are
in a constant struggle against each other, and for Them, a
few thousand years is but a moment of eternity. I suspect
that it was *meant* for your ancestor to find the Tahthlum,
meant for you to take it as a 'lucky piece,' and *meant* for you
to come here with it!" He gripped the boy by the shoulders.
"But even though the Powers can guide things in such a
way, they cannot make a person act in any way other than he
or she decides. It was always up to *you* to find the courage
and resolution to bring the Tahthlum to where it was
needed, here on the field of battle. If you had not had that
courage and resolution, the Tahthlum would never have
been used and the Fomoiri would have won a victory for
Darkness!"

"I had to come and help Moira," Rick mumbled in embarrassment, as if trying to explain.

"Ah, I understand now!" exclaimed Nion the Luchorpan,
who had been listening nearby to all of this. "Moira kept
saying that she felt she had to be here, within the Shadow,
even though she was deathly afraid. *Her* courage and resolution played a part in this, too! Her being here meant that
Rick had to make the choice to come and save her."

"Exactly," acknowledged Lair Bhan. "And when he made
that choice, which was the only decent and honorable
choice to be made, he also, without knowing it, chose to

110

become Light's Champion and the wielder of the Tahth-lum!"

The Danaan warriors were making way for a tall, silver-haired man whose helmet was ringed with a golden crown. As he came to where Rick, Moira, and the others stood, the two Druids bowed to him. "Rick and Moira," said Lair Bhan, "this is Fionn Mac Nuada, the *Ard Righ*—the High King—of the Danaan."

The High King bowed in a courtly manner to Moira, who quickly responded with a curtsy. He then extended a hand to Rick, who took it and bowed as the Druids had, a trifle self-consciously.

"Lad," said the king, "you were the greatest warrior on the field this day. You have saved the Danaan and saved the Middle Kingdom. Is there anything we can possibly do for you in return?"

Almost automatically Rick and Moira looked at each other in silent agreement. Rick looked back at the High King. "We want to go home, now," he pleaded.

The king gazed at them with compassion in his eyes. "I understand. We had hoped you would come with us back to Murias, where we might have a great feast of thanksgiving, and honor you both for what you have done. But I under-stand your need to go home as quickly as possible. This is not your world, and you are but youngsters who have been torn away from your mother and father and other loved ones." He looked toward Lair Bhan and Caithbad. "Can this be done quickly for them, Druids?"

"Quickly enough," said Lair Bhan. "But there is some-thing they must be told." He turned to the boy and girl. "Rick and Moira, *time* is different between your world and this one. A few moments here equal days in your world, and

111

a few days can equal years! In times past, people from your world have come here, stayed a short while, and gone back to find that years had passed, that all their family and friends were dead and gone, and that they were strangers in a changed world. We cannot let this happen to you! So Caithbad and I have worked out a way to return you into your world at the very instant before the Fomoiri appeared and you were snatched away from them and brought here. In other words, it will be as if you never came here at all. There will be no grief and worry for your parents, because for them as for you, it will be as if you had never been gone. The concern they are feeling now will be wiped out of their minds."

"That's great," Rick said. "I'd rather not have Mom and Dad go through a lot of worry, and I'm sure Moira feels the same about her folks. Thanks a lot, Lair Bhan."

"But you must understand," said the Druid, and there was sadness in his voice, "that you will have no memory of what happened here. You will not remember any of the great things you did, nor any of the terrors you bested. You will not remember any of those who became your friends here. For it will be as if all of this never happened!"

"That does not seem right," objected Faol. "They should know what great deeds they did here, and that they will be honored here forever. Can we not give them something to take back to their world that will enable them to re-member?"

Lair Bhan shook his head. "Actually, Faol, Caithbad and I worked this out so that they *wouldn't* remember. It is known that all those other people who came here from their world not only suffered the pain of finding their world changed when they went back to it but also suffered an agony of desire, all their lives, to return to the Middle Kingdom once again. The memory of the glamour and enchantment of this world causes a terrible yearning in a human heart. We do not want these two, our friends and saviors, to have to bear that curse!"

"Of course not," Faol instantly agreed. "But it is too bad. There ought to be some way we could give them a token of our friendship and esteem."

"I know a way!" crowed Nion. He winked at Rick and Moira. "I'll not tell you what it is, young ones, for you'd just be forgetting it anyway. It will be a surprise." He began to whisper to the High King, who bent down and listened attentively, nodding.

"Now that you know what is to happen, wouldn't you like to stay a little longer before leaving?" Lair Bhan asked of Rick and Moira. "We could at least have that feast the High King promised."

Again, Rick and Moira looked thoughtfully at each other. It was tempting, now that they knew their parents' grief and worry could be erased, and now that the danger and horror was over, to stay on for a while in this magical realm and enjoy the victory celebration. But Moira was troubled. "If I properly understand what you've explained," she said to Lair Bhan, "then the longer we stay here, the more time will pass in our own world. Doesn't that mean that our parents will just have that much more time to grieve for us, even though that grief will be wiped out once we go back?"

Lair Bhan pondered her question for a moment, then nodded. "Well, yes. I fear what you say is true. I regret I did not realize that."

113

"Then we should go back right away," said the girl firmly, glancing back at Rick. "I think we should spare our folks all the worry and sorrow we can."

"Right," the boy acknowledged.

"Your decision is wise and compassionate, as befits those who have helped the Light conquer the Darkness," Lair Bhan declared. "Very well then, say your last farewells and Caithbad and I will send you back."

Once again, Faol and Nion stepped forward to squeeze Rick's hand. "You'll be a great warrior when you're full grown," Faol declared. "As great as Cuchulainn!"

Nion was wiping his tearful eyes with his hood, which he had removed for the purpose. "I do hope ye'll somehow remember, lad," he said with a grin and a teary wink, "that it's Luchorpan—not leprechaun!"

Then they turned to Moira, who was surrounded by Teine, Foghar, and the other Danaan warriors who had entered the Shadow with her. "I want to thank all of you for trying to take care of me and for looking after me when the Fomoiri had us," said the girl tearfully.

Lair Bhan put an arm around Rick's shoulder. "If, somehow, you could have remained in the Middle Kingdom," he said with a wistful smile, "I'd have asked you to let me train you as a Druid. You could be a great one! I'll never forget how cleverly you bested Annis." He looked up. "Here come two others who want to say good-bye."

Neamh Suil landed gently on the boy's shoulder and bent toward his ear, uttering gentle clucking sounds. Roydeg pranced forward to drop his head and nuzzle Rick's other ear. With one finger Rick gently stroked the eagle's back, and with his other hand he caressed the unicorn's velvety nose. "I wish I didn't have to forget you," he said, tears

114

flowing unashamedly. "I've read wonderful stories about brave, magical animals, but I never dreamed I'd be lucky enough to really know two."

All too soon, the farewells were finished. The Danaan warriors, the Luchorpan, and the unicorn, with the eagle perched on his back, reluctantly drew away, leaving Rick and Moira and the two Druids in the center of a wide circle. Lair Bhan and Caithbad took up positions on each side of the youngsters, facing toward them. With both hands they raised their staffs horizontally over their heads and began to chant in unison. After a few moments it seemed to Rick and Moira as if the words were flowing and intertwining around them like living things. They were suddenly aware that the scene they were looking at was fading, and the shouts of final farewell from the crowd surrounding them echoed as if from a distance.

Moira felt momentarily dizzy and put a hand to her head, as if to steady herself. Then the feeling passed and she dismissed it. Glancing back up at the crest of the *sidhe*, she realized that she and Rick could not be seen from the road, and peering about at the fields that bordered the meadow on which the *sidhe* stood, she saw that they were empty, without a person in sight. For just a moment, thinking of the odd thing she and Rick had seen yesterday, and of the stories her father and brother had told at last night's supper, she felt a bit nervous, realizing that she and Rick were really quite isolated. Then she smiled sheepishly at her foolish fears. Nothing could happen!

Rick, standing halfway down the side of the *sidhe* from her, was looking hopefully about, his head jerking one way and another, and he reminded Moira so much of a chicken looking for a bug that she giggled. "I'm afraid there's nothing much to see," she told him. "This side of the *sidhe* looks just about like the other side."

He nodded and grinned, a trifle ruefully. "I guess I was hoping to find something—an old spear point or sword blade, maybe."

She giggled again. "If there ever were any such things lying about, they'd have been found by someone else long ago. Teachers and their classes and scientists and collectors and tourists have been poking and digging into this place for generations."

"I suppose so," he said. He shoved his hands into his pockets and started up the slope toward her, but stopped abruptly with a look of dismay on his face. "Hey, my lucky piece is gone! I must have lost it."

"What was it like?" Moira questioned. "I'll help you look for it."

"It was just a piece of reddish metal about the size of a golf ball, only with two flat sides," he told her. "I'm afraid it would only be a waste of time to look for it here. I had it when we started out this morning, so I could have lost it anywhere since." He shrugged. "I guess it doesn't matter. I don't think it ever really brought me any luck."

He continued on up the slope and together they began to climb down the other side. Halfway, the boy suddenly pitched forward and landed on all fours on the ground.

"My goodness," Moira exclaimed. "Are you all right?"

"I tripped over something," he complained, rising and rubbing his knee. "Felt like a rock sticking up." He turned to look for the cause of his tumble, and abruptly dropped to his knees and bent forward, peering intently. "Hey, this is

116

no rock. It looks like the corner of a box sticking out of the ground!"

"What?" She knelt beside him. "Why, you're right!"

Heedless of dirty fingernails and grass-stained clothing, they scrabbled and scratched and dug with their hands until they managed to tug and jiggle the object out of the soil in which it was partly buried. It was about the size of a one-pound box of chocolates, but it was made of a heavy, silvery-colored metal and was handsomely embossed and inscribed with intertwining patterns of vines and leaves.

"It's beautiful," said Moira in an awed whisper. "I wonder if there could be anything in it?"

"I'll see if I can get it open," said Rick. To his surprise, the lid lifted easily. Boy and girl gasped in unison as they saw the contents of the box.

There were two objects that at first glance appeared to be identical. They were round pendants about the size of a half dollar, suspended from small but sturdy chains, and while neither Rick nor Moira had ever chanced to see a piece of pure, natural gold they knew almost instinctively that this was what the pendants and chains were made of. Each youngster gingerly picked one up and scrutinized it.

"There are heads on them," marveled the girl. "Little heads of people and animals."

Circling the border of each disk was an identical series of tiny embossed heads, so beautifully sculpted that all features were distinct. Five were the heads of long-haired men wearing conical helmets, one was a long-haired man with a bare head, and one was a hooded, elflike man with a beard and a lumpy, potatolike nose. There was also the head of a fierce-eyed bird of prey, an eagle or hawk. And next to this

117

was a horselike head with a spiraled horn jutting from between its eyes—clearly, a unicorn. The heads were arranged so that they all looked inward from the side, toward a single large head that covered most of the center of each medallion. But unlike the others, these heads were not duplicated on each medallion. On the center of one disk was the head of a young boy, and the other featured the head of a young girl.

For minutes, Rick and Moira knelt side by side, silently studying the gleaming objects. Finally, Rick dared to utter the thought that was in both their minds.

"Moira—it's us," he said. For there was no doubt that the face of the boy on the one medallion was a perfect likeness of his face, and the face of the girl was clearly that of Moira.

"It can't be!" said Moira almost desperately. "This box must have been lying buried in the *sidhe* for thousands of years. It couldn't be us. It's just coincidence!" But then, after a moment she wailed, "It *is* us! But how could it be? Who made it? Who are these people and creatures that are looking at us so proudly and happily? What can it mean?"

"I wish I knew!" Rick gently stroked the heads of the unicorn and the bird of prey with his forefinger. "They're looking at us like they know us, so we should know them. But I sure never met any unicorn, or any of these others. They look like something out of a fairy tale."

"That's it!" Moira seized him by the arm. "They're Fairy Folk! Rick, it has something to do with that person we saw yesterday—the man in the black robe."

"He's not on here," objected the boy, indicating the medallion he held. "He wouldn't belong on here! These people and animals all look—nice. He seemed *evil!*"

"I think he *was* evil," Moira said. "And I think that you and I must have done something that helped these people against him. This is their way of thanking us."

"But what did we do?" protested Rick.

"I don't know. But I know that these are ours!" She slipped the chain with the pendant that bore her resemblance over her head and tucked the medallion into her collar. "There's a kind of law, I think, that any old thing that's found hereabouts, in the ground or in a ruin, is supposed to be taken to the museum in Cairwick. I'll give the box to Daddy and tell him where we found it, but let's not tell anyone about these pendants. They were meant for *us*."

"You're right," said the boy, adjusting the chain of his pendant around his neck. "Maybe someday we'll be able to figure out what happened, but at least we know that we did *something* that counted for enough so that these people and animals wanted to thank us. It's great. It's like having a medal!"

Together, they sauntered on down to where their bicycles stood against the stone fence. Mounting the vehicles, they sped off down the narrow road. A stray breeze passed over the *sidhe*, setting the grass in motion so that it fluttered from side to side, like thousands of tiny arms waving farewell.

About the Author

Author TOM MCGOWEN says: *"The Shadow of Fomor* was created for all young people who delight, as I do, in old-world fantasy. It is based on the war, fought with weapons and wizardry, between the heroic Tuatha De Danaan and the dreadful, monstrous Fomoiri, as recounted in age-old Irish legends. Woven into it are a number of Gaelic 'earth folk' such as a Luchorpan, Bodachs, Brollachans, and the terrible Annis Dubh, tales of which stretch back in time for thousands of years."

An editor for many years, Mr. McGowen has written more than thirty books for young people. He and his wife live in Norridge, Illinois. They have four children and ten grand-children.

THE SHADOW OF FOMOR

This book is about a boy who is visiting his cousin in Ireland. This girl's name is Moria. A strange passage zone opened by some men warps them into a fabled place where not only wizards but monsters exist. They are on an adventure to put to death the Shadow of the Fomor!!!!